Hiya!

Do you believe in magic? I do – not conjurer's tricks or scary spells, but the power of hopes, dreams and wishes. For me, the magic always seems strongest in beautiful, wild, middle-of-nowhere places, and that's why I've set *Scarlett* on the west coast of Ireland, one of my fave places ever.

Scarlett is an angry girl. Her life is just one long run of trouble, and when she is packed off to Ireland to live with her dad, Scarlett feels like she's been buried alive. Then she meets a mysterious boy, Kian, and the magic begins . . .

I hope you like *Scarlett*. It's a book for anyone who has ever felt angry, lost or misunderstood, a book for everyone who likes to dream. And whether you believe in wishes or not, they really can come true . . .

Best wishes,

 xxxx

www.cathycassidy.com

Cathy Cassidy

Scarlett

PUFFIN

PUFFIN BOOKS

Published by the Penguin Group
Penguin Books Ltd, 80 Strand, London WC2R ORL, England
Penguin Group (USA) Inc., 375 Hudson Street, New York, New York 10014, USA
Penguin Group (Canada), 90 Eglinton Avenue East, Suite 700, Toronto, Ontario, Canada M4P 2Y3
(a division of Pearson Penguin Canada Inc.)
Penguin Ireland, 25 St Stephen's Green, Dublin 2, Ireland (a division of Penguin Books Ltd)
Penguin Group (Australia), 250 Camberwell Road, Camberwell, Victoria 3124, Australia
(a division of Pearson Australia Group Pty Ltd)
Penguin Books India Pvt Ltd, 11 Community Centre, Panchsheel Park, New Delhi – 110 017, India
Penguin Group (NZ), 67 Apollo Drive, Rosedale, Auckland 0632, New Zealand
(a division of Pearson New Zealand Ltd)
Penguin Books (South Africa) (Pty) Ltd, 24 Sturdee Avenue, Rosebank, Johannesburg 2196, South Africa

Penguin Books Ltd, Registered Offices: 80 Strand, London WC2R ORL, England

puffinbooks.com

First published 2006
Published in this edition 2011
001 – 10 9 8 7 6 5 4 3 2 1

Set in Baskerville MT
Printed in Great Britain by Clays Ltd, St Ives plc

British Library Cataloguing in Publication Data
A CIP catalogue record for this book is available from the British Library

ISBN: 978-0-141-33891-0

www.greenpenguin.co.uk

MIX
Paper from
responsible sources
FSC
www.fsc.org   FSC™ C018179

Penguin Books is committed to a sustainable
future for our business, our readers and our
planet. This book is made from paper certified
by the Forest Stewardship Council.

Thanks . . .

Most of all, to Liam, Cal & Caitlin for their love, support, patience and first-reading skills – I couldn't have done it without you. Also to Mum, Dad, Andy, Lori, Joan and all of my fab family. Hugs and thanks to Catriona, Fiona, Mary-Jane, Sheena, Zarah, Mel and all my lovely friends – you're the best.

Special thanks to Elv, for uncovering the story I wanted to write all along, and to Francesca, Adele, Kirsten, Jo, Jodie, Sarah, Rebecca and all at Puffin for being so kind, clever and fab. Thanks to Darley Anderson for just being the best and coolest agent in the world, and to Julia, Lucie and all at the agency. Also to Paul for all his hard work on the website and Martyn for doing the sums!

A big thank you to Siobhan Daly, who helped so much and so patiently with my Irish research, and also to Dermott, Mickey, Tina and Maeve for their input. Thanks to Tania for the hair story, Hazel for the hazelly bits and Tara, who started me thinking in the first place.

I am in trouble, again. It's big trouble – the kind that requires urgent phone calls and whispered conversations in the school office while I sit on a plastic chair outside Mrs Mulhern's room, painting my fingernails black.

Sometimes I think that Greenhall Academy is more of a prison camp than a school. Mrs Mulhern is wasted as a Headmistress – with her charm, compassion and world vision she could be running Wormwood Scrubs. She's always banging on about how the fabric of society will just crumble away if you don't wear perfect school uniform and excel on the sports field and donate bars of soap and unwanted PlayStation games to the Third World, which is clearly kind of crazy.

Mrs Mulhern just loves rules, and I don't. That's the problem really.

I waft my fingernails about, trying to dry them, while Miss Phipps, the school secretary, runs around looking nervous and hassled. She digs out files and answers calls and gives me nasty looks with her lips all crinkled up like she's sucking a lemon.

'Scarlett,' she says sniffily, 'I still can't locate your mother. Her office say she's in a meeting and can't be disturbed. I've told them it's urgent, but they don't seem to care . . .'

'Too bad,' I sympathize, putting my feet up on the coffee table to see if she'll say anything. She doesn't. I think it's my red wedge sandals that scare her, or possibly the black skull-print ankle socks. She frowns and huffs and hides behind her PC screen.

I've been in trouble a million times before, and if there's one thing I've learnt it's that hanging your head in shame won't change a thing. They'll bawl you out anyway.

With a name like Scarlett, you cannot sneak through life blending into the background – people notice you, like it or not. Of course, they notice me even more these days, since I had my hair dyed the colour of tomato soup, but hey, why not? You can't fight destiny.

Mum once told me that red is nature's warning colour, signifying danger, trouble. It warns the other animals to back off, stay away. I like to think that my name and my hair colour are a little clue for the rest of the world to do just the same – back off and leave me alone. If they choose not to take notice of the warning, well, that's not my fault, is it?

It's past three by the time Mum appears. She stalks into the office in her swish grey suit and her spike-heeled shoes, her hair swept up in a bun with strands of expensive honey-blonde streaks falling delicately round her face. She kicks my feet off the coffee table with one pointy toe, drops her briefcase on to a chair and leans towards Miss Phipps.

'So,' she says in a tired voice. 'What's she done *this* time?'

Things move quickly after that. We're taken through to Mrs Mulhern's office and seated in front of her big, leather-topped desk. Miss Phipps brings in a tray of freshly brewed coffee and pours one for everyone except me before bustling back to the outer office. I don't even get a biscuit. I'm probably destined for solitary confinement and a diet of bread and water, if Mrs Mulhern has her way.

'I'm very sorry to have brought you here this afternoon – er, *Ms* Murray,' Mrs Mulhern begins. 'I'm afraid we've had another *incident*. I'm sure I don't need to tell you that Scarlett isn't settling in too well at Greenhall Academy. There have been countless problems, from somewhat minor breaches of the school-uniform code . . .'

She pauses to glower at my feet and hair.

'. . . To rather more serious issues, which, as you know have already resulted in two periods of exclusion from the school.'

'Yes, yes,' Mum responds. 'Just tell me what she's done.'

'The incident began with a demonstration in the school lunch hall,' Mrs Mulhern says. 'I believe Scarlett has recently become vegetarian?'

Mum rolls her eyes, exasperated.

'She was leafleting students as they came into the hall,' Mrs Mulhern continues. 'With these.'

She pushes a crumpled flyer across the desk at Mum, who picks it up between finger and thumb as though it might be contaminated. I'm proud of those leaflets – they really caused a stir. Personally, I think it was the crimson blood-splash motif that grabbed people's attention.

'The leaflet is just the tip of the iceberg,' Mrs Mulhern goes on. 'Some pupils were distressed, refusing to eat the meat-based meals, and the cook became a little upset . . .'

A little? That's a laugh. She was purple with rage, and when I tried to explain the links between a meat-based diet and high blood pressure, she said a few things that shocked even me. Are dinner ladies *supposed* to swear?

'Things got a little nasty,' Mrs Mulhern ploughs on. 'Chicken nuggets were thrown, and bottles of ketchup squirted all over the walls. It came to a head when Scarlett lifted up a large tray of Irish stew and threw it all over the lunch-room floor.'

'Oh dear,' says Mum.

'Oh dear, indeed,' echoes Mrs Mulhern. 'We have never had a riot at Greenhall Academy before. But then again, we have never had a pupil quite like Scarlett.'

'You can't blame her for the whole thing,' Mum says reasonably. 'She's certainly behaved badly, but –'

'But nothing,' Mrs Mulhern snaps. 'In the midst of the fray, Ms Murray, my cook was assaulted by your daughter.'

'She slipped!' I protest.

'She had to be taken to casualty, although fortunately nothing seems to be broken. She has also handed in her notice after more than twenty years at Greenhall.'

She's missed out the bit where the old bag chased me with a spatula and pelted me with semolina pudding, but I doubt whether these details will help my case any.

'Ah.' Mum sighs. 'I see.'

'I've no option but to exclude Scarlett from Greenhall Academy. A third exclusion, as you know, is a final one. We have a reputation to maintain, and we cannot tolerate incidents –

indeed, *pupils* – such as this. You will need to make alternative arrangements for Scarlett. I regret to tell you she is no longer a pupil at Greenhall Academy.'

'Whoop-de-doo,' I mutter, arranging the hem of my black school skirt so that it sits neatly across my knees.

'Mrs Mulhern,' Mum appeals, 'are you saying my daughter has been *expelled*?'

The Headmistress gives a slow, solemn nod.

'There's nothing I can say or do to make you reconsider?'

'Sadly, no,' Mrs Mulhern replies. 'Scarlett is a bright girl. She could have done well here, but she has major problems with authority – and with her temper. A broken home can affect young people in so many dreadful ways. Scarlett is quite one of the angriest twelve-year-olds I've ever come across.'

Mrs Mulhern stands up, offering a podgy, pink-taloned hand for Mum to shake. 'Have you ever thought that family counselling might be a solution?' she adds as an afterthought, and Mum drops the hand like a hot potato. Her face flushes with fury as she ushers me into the outer office.

'Everything OK, Ms Murray?' Miss Phipps calls sweetly, getting her own back at last for an afternoon wasted leaving urgent messages for my mother. 'Scarlett?'

Like she doesn't know. All afternoon, she's probably been typing up official forms and letters kicking me out of the school. She smirks at me from behind her PC.

Mum sails past as though Miss Phipps is invisible, but I find time to pause in the doorway and reveal my last and, possibly, my finest assault on the school-uniform rules. I've kept it secret for six whole weeks, which hasn't been easy, but hey, it's going to be worth it.

I open my mouth and stick my tongue out at Miss Phipps, wide enough and long enough for her to see the gold stud that pierces the middle of it. Then I close my mouth, smile sweetly and slam the door behind me.

Goodbye, Mrs Mulhern. So long, Miss Phipps. It's been fun.

Of course, getting kicked out of Greenhall Academy is no joke. Head teachers and school secretaries don't scare me, but Mum – well, that's a different story.

We travel home on the tube in stony silence, which is not good news. The first time I got excluded from Greenhall, Mum laughed and said that dyeing your hair green in the school toilets was hardly a criminal offence.

OK, I shouldn't have nicked that bottle of hydrogen peroxide from the chemistry lab, but I'd heard the stuff was used in hair dye, and I was trying to get a few cool blonde streaks. I didn't know it'd turn my hair into something that looked, felt and smelt like clumps of mouldering seaweed. Attractive – not.

Mum booked me into her swish Covent Garden hairdresser's and told them to cover up the mess, and I couldn't find a shade of brown I liked so I ended up going red. Mrs Mulhern nearly had a seizure when I walked back into school after my three-day exclusion with chin-length curls the colour of tomato ketchup.

The next time was worse. I had a scrap with my biology teacher, Miss Jessop, a turnip-faced dictator who tried to get me to cut a worm in half in class. I mean, who wouldn't object?

'I can't,' I'd argued, faced with a Tupperware box of worms to hand round to my fellow pupils. 'Seriously. It's against my religion. I'm . . . um, a Buddhist. I cannot harm any living animal.'

'Do it, Scarlett,' she'd barked. Her eyes were pinkish as she tried to stare me out, and her skin was pale and flabby. She looked kind of like an overgrown worm herself. 'Scalpels ready, class . . .'

I'd looked down into the Tupperware box of pink, squiggling creatures and even though they were the least cute and cuddly animals ever, I knew I couldn't do it. I couldn't let anyone else do it either. What makes it OK to chop up a worm but not a frog or a kitten or a person? It's just not right, is it?

'No way!' I'd shouted at Miss Jessop, shaking my fist at her. OK, I was still holding the scalpel, but there was no need for her to scream like that. I wasn't into cutting up worms, even outsize ones. I was on a rescue mission – I yanked open the first-floor window and flung the box of worms out. I had some vague idea they'd land on a patch of grass and wiggle away to live happily-ever-after, but sadly they landed on Miss Phipps, who was walking past below. I was in deep trouble – again.

'You threatened your biology teacher with a *knife*?' Mum asked me later, aghast.

'I didn't!' I protested. 'I may have had a scalpel in my hand, but . . .'

Mum closed her eyes and took a long breath in, and I could tell that this time she didn't see the funny side.

'You have to stop this,' she told me after that second exclusion. 'No more breaking the school rules, no more winding up the teachers. I'm sick of it, Scarlett. I want you to make a go of Greenhall. This is your last chance, OK? I mean it. Don't throw it away.'

I promised I wouldn't.

Oh well. It's not like I planned for this to happen, is it?

We get separated in the scrum at the Angel tube station, Mum striding on ahead, her lips set in a thin, hard line. Her mobile rings just as we reach the flat. It's her boss.

'No, no, I won't be back today,' she says. 'Something's come up. I'll work late tommorow to make up for it. Sure. No problem.'

She snaps the mobile shut and glares at me. I let myself into the shared hallway, then clomp up the stairs and let myself into the flat. I have my own key because Mum works late most nights. She follows me in, kicks off her shoes, chucks her briefcase down on the sofa.

'So,' she says at last. 'Another broken promise.'

I can't meet her gaze.

'Another last chance thrown away,' she continues. 'Another school glad to see the back of you. And now they're telling me you need counselling! Ha!'

I study my sandals, three inches of swirly-red wedge heels with pink-and-orange print uppers and criss-cross red-ribbon ties. There's a dull brown stain on one that may date back to the Irish-stew incident. I struggle to keep my expression blank.

'Scarlett, what's going on?' Mum explodes suddenly. 'What are you trying to do? Get chucked out of every school in London?'

I think that's a bit unfair. There are probably hundreds of schools in London I haven't been chucked out of yet.

'I'm disappointed in you, Scarlett. You promised me you'd work on that temper, and there you go again, worse than ever, attacking a school cook –'

'She started it!' I protest. 'And anyway, I didn't attack her, she slipped.'

Mum ignores me. 'This is a new personal best, even for you,' she snarls. 'Four months, you lasted at Greenhall. It's a joke!' But neither of us is laughing.

'I didn't mean it –' I begin, but she cuts me short.

'No, you never do. You don't mean it, and I try to be understanding, I give you a fresh start – and you throw it back in my face, Scarlett, every single time! Five schools in two years! Are you proud of that?'

Maybe I am, in a funny kind of way.

'It's only five schools because you sent me away,' I point out. 'You got sick of me and packed me off to Nan's. She got sick of me and packed me off to Uncle Jon's, and then he decided he'd had enough too and here I am back with you. Don't you think that would make me just a tiny bit angry, Mum? Don't you see that?'

'You know why I sent you to your nan's,' Mum growls.

I shake my head. Can there ever be a good reason for sending your eleven-year-old daughter miles and miles away to live with people she only ever sees at Christmas? I don't think so.

'You're out of control!' Mum rages. 'You're a selfish, destructive little troublemaker! I work hard trying to make a nice home for you. When was the last time I had a holiday? When was the last time I really got to relax? I work hard, Scarlett, and my career is taking off!'

'Lucky you,' I say sulkily.

'Don't I buy you nice things?' she rants on. 'The clothes you like? CDs, DVDs, Xbox games? You get a good allowance. What more do you want?'

I laugh out loud. A life? A family? But you can't argue with Mum when she gets like this. You just have to ride out the storm.

'I drop everything each time you get into trouble,' she says. 'I talk to your snotty teachers and tell them you'll change, try harder, toe the line. But you won't, will you? You just couldn't care less!'

I shrug, switch off, let it all wash over me. Mum sits down suddenly, and covers her face with one perfectly manicured hand.

'I don't know you any more,' she says. 'I don't know who you are.'

This makes me feel bad.

'Get to know me then,' I tell her. 'It's not so difficult.' I give her a shaky grin, but she's not buying.

'I meant it, Scarlett, when I said that Greenhall was your last chance,' Mum says. 'I can't give you the time and attention you need, you've made that very clear. I've tried, but it's just not working.

Five schools in two years, and every one of them was glad to see the back of you. Your so-called friends are a nightmare, your behaviour just gets worse and worse. Well, not any more. I've had enough.'

'Enough of me?' I ask in a very small voice.

Mum closes her eyes and lets her head fall back against the sofa. She takes a deep breath in. 'You need to get away from here, make a fresh start. It's something I've been thinking about ever since the scalpel incident, and the tongue piercing.'

'Not Nan's again?' I protest. 'That didn't work, you said so. Mum, I was so lonely . . .'

'Not Nan's,' she says. 'It's time to try something different,'

'Boarding school?' I ask in a whisper. 'Please, Mum, not that!'

She shakes her head, pulls the clips from her hair and shakes it free. My mum looks at me, all rumpled honey-blonde hair and cool blue eyes, and I'm scared.

'You leave me no option, Scarlett,' she says. 'I've done all I can. I know it's something we agreed we'd never do, but really you leave me no choice. You have to learn that your actions have consequences. I've made my decision. No arguing, no discussion. It's decided. OK?'

'What, Mum?' I ask. 'Just tell me.'

There is silence in the flat, except for the ticking of the clock, the thump of my heart.

'You're going to live with your dad,' she says.

World War III breaks out in our flat then.

'No,' I tell Mum quietly. 'Seriously, no. No, *no*, *NO!*'

She puts her hands over her ears and closes her eyes, and leans back on the sofa like she hasn't a care in the world.

'You promised!' I say. 'You said I'd never have to see him again, not after what he did to us! He left us, Mum, he walked away. You said he was scum! You said we were well shot of him, that we'd make like he'd never existed!'

'That was two years ago, Scarlett,' Mum sighs. 'Things change. I was angry, I shouldn't have said those things.'

But she did say them, and all of them are true. My dad left us, and I'll never forgive him for that. He walked out of our lives and didn't look back, and I don't care if I never see him again as long as I live. There is no way on this earth I am going to live with him. Or *her*.

'You're kidding, right?' I say. 'You hate him as much as I do. He dumped us – to be with that witch Clare and her stupid, snotty kid. He replaced you, Mum. He replaced *me*.'

'It's decided, Scarlett,' Mum says.

I lose it then and my voice builds up to a scream. All kinds of stuff is tumbling out of my mouth – bad stuff, mean stuff, spiteful stuff. She's not listening, though. She never listens. Sometimes I don't think she'd take any notice if I burst into flames right in front of her.

I kick over the coffee table, still littered with this morning's cereal bowls and empty glasses. A pool of juice slides out from the tipped-up carton and stains the cream-coloured carpet. Mum doesn't even blink.

I pick up my school bag and hurl it against the wall with a satisfying thud. A framed school photo of me aged five, all gap-toothed grins and neatly pressed uniform, clatters to the floor. The girl in that photo is happy, hopeful, without a care in the world. I can't even remember what it was like to be her. I stamp on the picture with my red wedge sandals until the glass shatters, and then I rip the photo into little pieces.

Someone knocks loudly on the door, and Mum snaps to attention and goes to answer it. She doesn't have a problem hearing other people, only me.

'Is everything all right?' asks the man from downstairs. 'I could hear lots of shouting and crashing about. Is something wrong?'

'We're fine,' says Mum smoothly. 'Just a little disagreement.'

'Well,' says the man, frowning, 'OK. But keep it down, could you?'

He turns away, and I fling a sheepskin cushion at the back of his head. Mum grabs it before it hits home and calmly puts it back on the sofa, then moves on to pick up the coffee table, and carries the dirty dishes out to the kitchen. She mops up the orange-juice stain, and wraps the shards of shattered glass and tattered bits of photograph in newspaper to put in the bin.

She is very efficient, my mother. She covers my tracks, hides the evidence, tidies up the mess. It's like I never got mad in the first place.

Pretty soon, there'll be no trace of me left here at all.

Everyone has choices, according to Mum. Life chucks a bunch of stuff at us, stuff we have no control over, but we can decide how to handle it all. We shape our lives with the choices we make.

What a load of rubbish. Life isn't fair – you think it's going to be one way, and then it tips in the other direction and everything's upside down.

How do you make choices when everything's turned to dust in your hands? It's impossible.

It's Tuesday night. Five days have gone by, and we've had all the talks, the rows, the tantrums. We've been round and round in circles till there's nowhere left to go.

'This is the best option,' Mum says gently, helping me to pack my suitcase. It's the same case I took to Nan's, the same one I took to Uncle Jon's, and just looking at it gives me an ache in the pit of my stomach.

'Best for you or me?' I ask, but I already know the answer. Best for her. She's the one with the choices, she's the one calling the shots. I just get pushed around from place to place, like a bit of unwanted luggage.

'Scarlett, please,' says Mum. 'We have to be positive about this.'

'I am,' I tell her. 'Positive I'll never forgive you.'

She folds up my red Chinese dress, and a pair of black parachute trousers. 'It's all about attitude,' she tells me. 'Lose that chip on your shoulder, stop feeling sorry for yourself. None of that helps, Scarlett. You act like the whole world's against you.'

'Not the whole world, just you,' I snap, stuffing rolled-up tights and neon plastic bracelets into the case.

'You made your choices,' she repeats. 'You knew

the score. D'you think I'll just stand by and let you mess up your entire education? Greenhall was your last chance, Scarlett, you knew that. Don't blame me for the fact that you blew it.'

'How come you're so hard?' I ask her.

'Maybe I learnt it from you,' she says. 'Too bad. I've done my best, and maybe it wasn't good enough, but I'm *not* going to stand by and watch you throw your life away.'

'No, you're packing me off to the middle of nowhere so you won't have to. You won't even have to hear my screams,' I point out. 'It was bad enough being parcelled off to Milton Keynes to stay with Nan, and then to Uncle Jon's, but this time we won't even be in the same country. You can't make me go there, Mum. You might as well bury me alive.'

'Scarlett, it's Ireland, not Outer Mongolia,' she says.

'Please don't, Mum,' I beg. 'I'll be different, I'll be better, I won't break the rules or get into fights, I promise. One last, last chance. I won't let you down. Don't send me away, OK?'

She pulls out a drawer, folding summer shorts and little black vest-tops into the case.

'Not yet then, OK?' I appeal, changing tack. 'I can go in the summer holidays, ready for the autumn term. Not now!'

'Your dad's expecting you,' she says, and my heart sinks to my boots. 'He's enrolled you in the local school, sorted out a room for you, everything. There's no point delaying things.'

I turn away, lift a neatly folded jumper from the bed and hug the soft black mohair against my skin.

'C'mon, Scarlett,' she says, putting an arm round my shoulders. 'The break will do us good. We can write, and email, and call, can't we? Look – I bought you a present!'

Mum is good at presents. She is a top advertising executive and she earns a small fortune, so money is not a problem. In spite of myself, I take the box-shaped parcel, tear off the silver tissue paper. It's a mobile, a new colour-screen model with video messaging. A week ago I'd have squealed and laughed and told her I loved it, but today I just feel empty, hollowed out, and I can't even find the words to say thanks.

A mobile phone, so my mum can keep in touch when she sends me to live a million miles away, with the enemy. Hundreds of miles, anyhow. Am I meant to be grateful?

'Give it a try, Scarlett?' she says. 'See how it goes? Your dad still loves you. I was the one he wanted to leave, not you, never you. I was wrong to let you think otherwise, but I was hurt, I guess, and I wasn't thinking straight. He's so happy that you're coming over, really he is.'

'This is such a bad idea,' I whisper, sinking down on to the bed beside the suitcase. 'Don't make me do it.'

'Choices, Scarlett,' says Mum. 'I'll miss you like mad, but I think it's for the best. It's a fresh start. A last, last chance, if you like. Don't waste it. Don't throw it away. OK?'

'But I hate him,' I protest. 'Seriously.'

Mum puts her arms round me and hugs me tight, and I think of the smiling face in the torn-up photograph, the little girl who didn't know her dad was going to leave and pull her whole world to pieces as he went. I take a deep breath in, my voice all raggedy and sad. 'I hate you too.'

Mum holds me tighter, rocking me, stroking my back. 'I know, sweetheart,' she whispers into my hair. 'I know.'

The picture on my passport shows a brown-haired girl with bunches and sparkly eyes, and the girl at the airport check-in desk squints at it hard, trying to make the connection between that kid and me. I scowl at her, stony-faced, and she swallows hard, checking in my bag without another word.

Mum gets permission to come through to the departures lounge with me, because twelve is kind of young to be on the loose in an airport, on your own. I think she just wants to be sure I get on that plane.

'Now, Scarlett, your dad doesn't know you got your tongue pierced,' Mum says briskly. 'Let's face it, he'd have a fit if he knew – blame me, probably. How about you take it out, put it away for a couple of days?'

I grin, tapping the gold stud against my teeth. If Dad's going to hate my piercing, it's staying for sure.

'Well, how about you just keep your mouth shut

for a few days?' Mum suggests. 'First impressions count. No sense asking for trouble, is there? For me, Scarlett?'

'OK.' I sigh.

'I've packed some goodies for your lunch,' Mum says as we walk up to the departure gate. 'Your dad will meet you by the main exit at Knock Airport. Just collect your suitcase and go through, OK? Scarlett, don't be like that – you know it's for the best.'

I nod listlessly. I don't have the strength left to argue. It's a fight I can't win, a risk I can't take. I don't want to fall apart, right here in the middle of the Stansted Airport departures lounge, with snotty businessmen in pinstriped suits looking on. That would never do.

The flight is called, and everyone clumps together at the gate, waiting to board the plane. I catch Mum looking at her watch. She collars a passing cabin-crew girl and asks her to keep an eye on me until the plane lands at Knock. The girl smiles and nods, then catches sight of my scowl and pales a little.

'I'll ring you,' Mum says. 'Sweetheart, don't let me down this time. Be good. Remember, it's your last, last chance.'

She hugs me, swiftly, lightly, with an air-kiss on each cheek. Then she steps back, brushing an imaginary speck of dust off her caramel-coloured trousers. 'Speak to you later, sweetheart. Take care!' She turns and strides away, tan shoulder bag swinging. I watch until she is out of sight in the crowd, but she doesn't look back.

The cabin-crew girl is leading me through the corridor, down a flight of steps and out on to the tarmac. I stumble up the steps and on to the plane, taking my seat in a trance. Two elderly ladies who've been scooshing themselves with the duty-free perfume squeeze in next to me, offering me a boiled sweet to suck during take-off.

I should have made a run for it while I had the chance, because I'm stuck now, no escape. There's a sad feeling in my chest, a cold, empty ache that won't go away.

I crunch my boiled sweet and try to unzip my rucksack, but my fingers feel numb and clumsy. It's a new rucksack, a red, fun-fur circle with sticky-up ears, googly eyes and a zigzag, growly mouth – a last-minute present from Mum. I'd have loved to throw it back at her, but of course, I didn't. It's cool, so I ignore the fact that it's also a bribe.

The cabin crew show us what to do in case of an emergency, and I find myself wishing the plane would plummet down into the middle of the Irish Sea, because then they'd be sorry they made me go. Maybe.

We taxi along the runway, the cabin crew take their seats and suddenly we're hurtling along so fast I just about choke on my boiled sweet. The plane tilts upwards, climbing, and just for a minute I forget to be scared because we're flying now, up through the clouds, higher and higher, until the stuff down below looks tiny and faraway, like toys scattered across a musty green carpet.

I check out the packed lunch Mum's provided. Rolls, crisps, apple pie and pop, all from the Marks & Spencer food hall. The rolls are chicken salad. Did she really not remember that I'm vegetarian now, or does she think that chicken doesn't count? 'Not another silly phase,' she said when I first told her. 'I think you do it just to irritate me!'

Mum's packed a magazine too, one with lots of pictures of ponies and kittens that I haven't bought since I was ten.

We're flying over the sea now, and the ladies sitting next to me are reading magazines full of knitting patterns and cake recipes and heartwarming stories about country doctors. The sad feeling in my chest has become an ache. It's scary, I swear. If I didn't know better, I'd say there was a big splinter of glass lodged just above my heart, pressing down, making everything hurt. I can barely breathe.

I lean back against the soft plush seat and close

my eyes. When I open them again, my neck feels sore, my face stiff, and outside the plane the view has changed to mottled green and grey.

'All right, pet?' one of the old ladies asks. 'Nearly there.'

I fish around in the rucksack for my hand mirror. My hair falls round my face in dark red ringlets; my eyes are ringed with smudgy black. It's a good disguise. I don't look scared, I look scary, and that's the way I like it.

The plane is dipping down through the clouds, banking and turning and finally swooping in to land with a roaring, whooshing sound that has my heart pounding.

Then the cabin crew are wishing us a safe onward journey, and we file off the plane and troop across to the terminal building and along to the hall where you get your luggage. It takes ages for the conveyor belt to start up, so I sit on a bench and ring Mum on my mobile. I can't get a signal for ages, and when I do she has her mobile switched off. I call the office, but Alima, her secretary, says Mum is out all afternoon.

I write a text message. *Kidnapped and sent 2 Ireland. Please help.* I press send.

The conveyor belt creaks into life and luggage starts tumbling down on to the carousel, black bags and brown bags and fancy plaid bags, suitcases and rucksacks and finally my old case. I let it circle the carousel three times before dragging it off the conveyor belt and on to a trolley, and by then all the other passengers have gone.

It's only when I turn to start pushing the trolley that I see a familiar figure in the distance, watching me. I miss my footing for a moment, and have to grab on to the trolley. It's just these stupid sandals – walking on three-inch wedges is never a picnic.

He's coming towards me. There's nowhere I can hide, and that's not fair, because Mum said he'd meet me by the main exit. He's not allowed to turn up here, when I'm still tired and rumpled from the journey. I am not ready for this.

'Scarlett!' he says. 'I waited a while and you didn't appear, so I thought I'd come and find you. Couldn't wait to see you!'

I fix my face into a cold, blank mask and refuse to look at him. He touches my arm and I shake him off furiously. How dare he touch me? How dare he?

'OK, Scarlett, OK,' he says softly, the way you'd talk to a startled pony or an unruly puppy. He grabs my case and swings it off the trolley, striding through the hall and out to the car park where his old Morris Traveller is sitting, a stupid, ugly, ancient car from about a hundred years ago. It actually has strips of wood round the windows and doors, like something out of *The Flintstones*.

He dumps my suitcase on to the back seat, so I have no choice but to sit in the front beside him. The car smells of warm leather and Polo mints, just like it always did. He turns the key and the engine shudders to life, sounding like a small tractor and moving only very slightly faster. It is easily the most embarrassing car in the whole universe.

'Right then,' says Dad. 'Let's go home.'

Think of a girl, a skinny, grinny ten-year-old girl with curly brown hair and freckles and the kind of giggle you can hear a mile away. That was me. I was pretty, I was popular, I worked hard at school – yes, *me*. Seriously.

I was pretty much your typical middle-class, over-achieving London kid, with classes every night of the week, from karate and keyboards to drama and ballet.

I lived in a three-bedroom house in Islington with Mum and Dad, and I dreamt of having my own pony, shiny-black with a white blaze on its forehead. I planned to turn the garage into a stable, turn the backyard over to grass. I was going to call my pony Star and braid its mane with ribbons and feed it hay that smelt of summer and happiness. Together, we'd win horse shows and races and cross-country trials, collecting rosettes and trophies.

'One day, Scarlett,' Dad used to say. 'When we

live in the country. Imagine it – chickens, a veggie patch, room for a pony . . .'

'Don't encourage her,' Mum would snap. 'We're not moving anywhere. You can't have a pony in central London, Scarlett. How about a hamster?' In the end I got two rabbits, Coco and Fudge, who lived in a hutch in the garden.

Mum worked late most nights even then, but Dad was self-employed, so that didn't matter. He ran a web-design business, working from home, so he was always around to pick me up from school, take me to classes, heat up frozen pizza if my mates came round for a sleepover and pretend not to notice if we sat up past midnight, eating ice cream in bed.

He was a cool dad – embarrassing, sure, but cool. I didn't mind the Morris Traveller back then, not even when Dad called it Woody in front of my mates and pretended it was farting every time the engine backfired. I didn't mind when we went to eat out and he sat at the dinner table balancing a spoon on the end of his nose, not even that time it fell off into his soup and splashed his shirt with Cream of Tomato and Basil. So what?

I was just about the luckiest girl alive, and I didn't even know it.

Dad moved out just after my tenth birthday. He'd met someone else, he said, an Irish woman called Clare who made handmade soap out of herbs and spices and bits of grated lemon rind. Eye of newt and mouldy fingernail clippings, more like. If ever there was a witch, it had to be Clare.

Clare wanted a website to help sell her stuff. It shouldn't have been a big job, but she needed help to photograph the stuff, help to write the captions, help to choose the artwork and lettering.

'I hope she's paying for all this extra work,' Mum sniffed, after Dad spent a whole Saturday styling and photographing a bunch of speckled soaps that looked like they were made of cooking fat and boiled-up twigs. 'She's taking advantage of you.'

Dad just laughed and said that Clare was a nice woman, and that she deserved a bit of help.

'Why can't she help herself?' Mum had snapped.

I thought Mum was being a bit mean, but that's just what Clare did. She helped herself – to my dad. I didn't even see it coming.

'It's not that I don't love you any more,' Dad said to me before he left. 'I do. I always will, Scarlett. It's just that things aren't working out with your mum. They haven't been for a while.'

I tried to believe him, even as I watched him pack. 'Can't you try a bit harder then?' I wanted to know. 'It might just be a bad patch. Gill's parents had one of those, and *they're* all right. You just have to bring home flowers and chocolates and hold Mum's hand a bit more.'

'Scarlett, love, it's too late for all that,' he said.

'Well, you don't have to *leave*,' I argued. 'You can still live here, can't you? We're your family, you should be here, with us. Tell that stupid Clare woman to go away.'

Like *that* was ever going to happen.

'Scarlett, love, I can't,' he told me. 'I don't want to. I'm sorry.'

Sorry? That didn't really cut it, for me. He moved out of our house and into Clare's, and Mum and I were history. I got to see him every Sunday, and we'd trudge around the British Museum or sit in McDonald's, picking at our Happy Meals and wondering how it got to this.

'Clare's nice,' he said to me one week. 'You'd like her. Why not come over next week, get to know her a bit?'

'She's a witch,' I huffed. 'I hate her.'

'Scarlett, you don't even know her.' He sighed. 'Give her a chance. She's a good woman. She has a little girl – Holly, she's seven. Nice kid. I'm sure you'd get on . . .'

A little girl? My world crumbled.

I cried so hard when he dropped me home that night that Mum said we should cut the meetings to every other week. It was too upsetting, too disruptive. Pretty soon, we were down to once a month.

It doesn't have to be the end of the world when your parents split up, I know, but it was for me. It felt like my whole life was sliding away from me. I didn't go to karate and keyboards and drama and ballet any more, because Dad wasn't there to take me. I stopped dreaming of ponies and I went to after-school club till Mum finished work and could pick me up. There were no more sleepovers, no more embarrassing moments with farting cars or spoons balanced on noses.

I sat in my room and watched the grass grow on the lawn, the weeds sprout through the cracks in the garden path. When Mum told me we were selling the house so she and Dad could split the profits, I didn't even care.

I cleared away four bin bags of old clothes and toys, books about ponies, bits and pieces of my childhood. Dad called round late one night and loaded them up in the Morris Traveller to take to the charity shop.

Mum made me give Coco and Fudge to the kids next door, because you can't keep rabbits in a flat, and I still wonder if those kids remember that Coco hates apples, or that Fudge loves it when you scratch her behind her ears. Probably not.

We packed up our stuff and moved to the flat,

and then the divorce came through and Dad and Clare got married in a registry office in Camden. Soon after, they all moved to Ireland, to some dump called Kilimoor, in Connemara where Clare grew up, and the very last shreds of hope died inside me.

That was that. It wasn't enough just to leave us, replace us, he had to move a million miles away and put the Irish Sea between us. Well, fine. If he wanted to act like we didn't exist any more, I could do the same. I stopped answering his emails, stopped taking his calls. I threw his cards and letters into the bin. I wiped him out of my life, the way he'd wiped us out of his.

I didn't need him. Not even when I got into trouble at school, not even when Mum packed me off to Nan's in Milton Keynes for the very first fresh start. Not even when Nan said she couldn't cope and sent me on to Uncle Jon's, or when he said I was a spoilt little brat with violent tendencies and packed me off back to Mum. Families, hey? Don't you just love 'em?

My dad pulled my life to bits and trampled all over it with his size-ten boots. I need him like I need a hole in the head, or maybe even less.

The journey to Kilimoor is hell on wheels. The Morris Traveller cruises at forty-five miles an hour, and pretty soon there's a mile-long queue of traffic behind us, waiting to overtake. I wouldn't be surprised to see small children on tricycles whooshing past us.

'It's a bit of a drive,' Dad says. 'I thought it'd give us a chance to catch up.'

I don't *think* so. We drive through open countryside, past dozens of smart ranch-style bungalows fronted by pillars and tall gateposts topped with stone eagles and lions. I maintain a gloomy silence.

I do a double-take when we pass gateposts topped with stone cats, lop-eared rabbits and, finally, what looks very much like penguins.

'Different, isn't it?' Dad smirks.

It's different, all right. It's a foreign country, and a crazy one. As well as the loony gateposts, I spot several garden shrines with brightly painted statues of the Virgin Mary, and one swish modern bungalow with a trio of ancient, rusting tractors arranged decoratively on the lawn. There are endless ruined cottages overgrown with ivy, green post-office vans and alarming yellow signposts written in some kind of foreign language. Even the car number plates are weird.

'The Irish have their own unique style,' Dad says as we chug past a pink-and-orange painted building that seems to be half pub, half petrol station, with a sideline in hanging baskets and sacks of coal. An old man in a flat cap and a tweedy waistcoat is snoozing on a deckchair by the elderly petrol pumps, while a tethered goat chomps through one of the hanging baskets. I peer back over my shoulder to get a better look, and see that the building has only half a roof.

'Interesting, huh?' Dad grins.

I pretend I am a million miles away, somewhere quiet and sane and peaceful where there is no crazy landscape, no smell of leather and Polo Mints, no stupid questions.

'You have to talk to me sometime, y'know,' Dad says.

'Wanna bet?' I retort, then wince because he's tricked me into answering. Typical.

The car journey takes forever and then some. I close my eyes to discourage further conversation, and when I open them, the landscape is different, wilder. We've turned off the main road. We're clattering through small, twisty lanes edged with tall hedges, starry with purple-pink flowers. At some places we have to slow down because there are chickens on the road, and all around us hills and mountains rise up, big, silent, spooky.

'This is Kilimoor,' Dad says as the Morris Traveller wheezes through a sleepy village tucked into a fold in the mountains. There's a teeny school, a church and a bunch of time-warp type shops that look like they've been painted by a colour-blind toddler with a palette of violently clashing colours.

The main street is strung out along the most desolate stretch of coastline I've ever seen in my life. A huge, grey ocean rolls away into the distance, brooding beneath a sullen sky.

'Amazing, isn't it?' Dad grins. 'It's like being on the edge of the world.'

It looks like the back of beyond to me, but slightly less exciting.

'The cottage isn't actually *in* the village,' Dad says as we head back into the open countryside. 'It's about seven miles on, near Lough Choill, woods and fields and hills all around. Very peaceful.'

Peaceful? I want to scream.

We drive past bleak moorland where big chunks

of ground have been sliced away and stacked in heaps. 'They still cut peat from the land, the way they have for hundreds of years,' Dad tells me. 'Just wait till you smell your first peat fire. Connemara is a magical place, Scarlett – not like the twenty-first century at all.'

'More like the Jurassic Age?' I ask sweetly. 'Mmm, I can tell.'

We crawl onwards, up twisting mountain lanes, dipping down into a vast, empty valley. The houses fizzle out, except for a tumbledown cottage with donkeys in the garden and a selection of derelict ruins overgrown with ivy.

Then, through a stand of trees, I glimpse a long strip of silver-blue water that glints in the afternoon sun.

'That's Lough Choill,' Dad tells me. 'Lough is the Irish word for lake – it sounds just the same as the Scottish word *loch*.'

'Fascinating.' I scowl.

'The name means lake of the hazel tree,' Dad says. 'There's an old hazel at the tip of the lough that marks a holy well or a spring or something. People still come to see it. It's supposed to have magical properties, according to local legend.' I fake a yawn, and Dad abandons the running commentary.

We're quite close to the water now. Lough Choill looks cold and still and timeless, rimmed on the far shore with silver birch trees that seem to dip their toes in the water. Beyond the woodland, a huge, gaunt hillside rises up, smudged with heather and gorse.

'Almost there,' says Dad. We drive round the tip of the lough, turning off into a lane that's so skinny it might not even qualify as a footpath back in London. There is grass growing up through the middle of the road. Unreal.

The car shudders to a halt outside a whitewashed cottage with red-painted windows and climbing roses all round the doorway.

'Well,' says Dad. 'This is it.'

The cottage looks like it's escaped from a picture postcard. A stone workshop with a tin roof stands behind the cottage, and strewn across the neatly mown lawn in front are a pink bike, a pogo stick, an abandoned Bratz doll. A couple of chickens mooch about in the flower beds, and there's even a neat vegetable plot. It looks like Dad got his country-cottage dream, anyhow.

A tyre swing hangs from a tree, swaying gently in the breeze. My mouth sets into a grim line.

Dad grabs my suitcase and grins at me, that old lopsided smile I know so well. 'Don't be nervous,' he tells me. 'They don't bite.'

Too bad, I think. *Because I do.*

*

The fridge is crowded with magnetic letters that spell out 'Welcome, Scarlett', and the kitchen smells of roast meat and gravy. Yuk. I drop my eyes to the floorboards, scowling.

'Scarlett, this is Holly,' Dad says, and my eyes flicker upwards against my will. Holly looks about nine, with mouse-brown hair scraped back into pigtails. She is setting the table with plates, glasses and cutlery, and she looks nervous but friendly, like she's pleased to see me. Weird.

'Wow,' she says, eyes flicking from my hair to my rucksack to my red wedge sandals. 'Wow! I'm so glad you're here. I can't believe I've really got a sister at last!'

'I am *not* your sister,' I say. Obviously she's not very bright.

'Stepsister then.' Holly shrugs. 'Mum's done us a roast dinner specially – lamb and mint sauce and roasted potatoes! It's a celebration!'

'I'm vegetarian,' I snap. 'Didn't anyone tell you?'

Holly's face falls.

'Your mum didn't mention that,' Dad says, frowning. 'Pity. Well, I could open a tin of tuna . . .'

'No meat, no fish,' I say coldly.

'Right. No, of course. Cheese then? And some of the vegetables?'

I shrug, stony-faced.

'I've always wanted to be veggie,' Holly chirps.

'At least, I've thought about it. You can tell me all about it, Scarlett. You'll be sharing my room – it's going to be cool!'

Yeah, right. I look at Dad and he raises one eyebrow shiftily.

'It's just one of several possible options, room-wise,' he says.

'No,' I correct him. 'It *isn't*.'

'And you're at my school.' Holly beams. 'Isn't that the best? I've told everyone all about you.'

Oh yeah? No pressure, then. She is nuts, clearly. I shake my head.

'You're at the primary school,' I point out, quite patiently, I think.

'Yes, in Kilimoor!' She grins. 'I'm just finishing Third Class, but of course, it's just a one-teacher school, so we're all mixed in together. Our teacher's called Miss Madden.'

'I'm twelve,' I tell Holly. 'Nearly thirteen. I'll be going to the secondary school, OK? With the big kids.'

Holly frowns and looks at Dad.

'Actually, Holly's right,' Dad says sheepishly. 'The system is slightly different in Ireland. You'll be at the primary school until the end of term, and then in September you'll go on to the secondary in Westport. It's not a step backwards or anything – both of the other kids in Sixth Class are the same age as you.'

42

'Both?' I echo. 'There are only *two* other kids my age?'

'I've got lots of tips on settling in,' Holly babbles on. 'The tricky bit is when someone says something in Gaelic, but of course we learn it at school anyway, so you'll soon catch on.'

'Gaelic?' I wrinkle my nose.

'You know, Irish. We have to study it,' Holly explains. 'I'll teach you a bit. *Céad Míle Fáilte!* It means a hundred thousand welcomes!'

A hundred thousand butterflies settle suddenly in my tummy. I have a bad feeling about this place, a very bad feeling. I sink down on to a kitchen chair.

Primary school. Can it get any worse? It can, of course.

A small, plump woman with fair wavy hair and witchy blue eyes comes into the kitchen, wiping her hands on a big floral apron. Clare.

'Oh, Scarlett, hi.' She beams, squeezing my arm. 'We're so glad to have you here, really! You're very welcome, and I know you're going to love it here just as much as we do.'

I sit still, frozen, speechless. I can't think of a single clever put-down. Why didn't they warn me? Why didn't they say?

Why didn't someone tell me Clare was pregnant?

I didn't sleep last night. I lay curled up on a rickety iron bed under a lumpy patchwork quilt, in a poky room with sky-blue walls and a border of nursery-ryhme characters. At least they had the decency to take the cot away.

I called Mum a dozen times last night, but she wasn't answering her phone. I left voicemail messages and texts, but she didn't call back. I'm on my own.

I'm up early, washed and dressed in my Greenhall Academy uniform. I choke down my breakfast, some kind of muesli that looks just like the dry food I used to feed to my pet rabbits. Clare looks pleased, Dad looks nervous and Holly looks slightly disappointed.

'You look very smart, Scarlett,' Dad says. 'It's great that you're trying to make a good impression.'

Trying? I can be very trying, when I put my mind to it.

'Ah,' he says, glimpsing my swirly wedge sandals

beneath the table. 'No school shoes?' His cheeks flush pink and I know he's not going to challenge me. 'Right. Well then, girls, off you go. Don't want to miss that school bus. Have a good day. I've spoken to Miss Madden, Scarlett – she knows all about you.'

All about me? That's scary. Holly and I head out into the lane, then mooch up to the crossroads for the bus.

'Are you nervous?' Holly wants to know. 'I was, my first day here. Everything was different, but now I love it. It's miles better than London, seriously. You'll be fine.'

'I'm not nervous,' I tell her. 'I've been to five schools in two years – I know all the tricks. What's to worry about?'

'Five schools?' Holly asks, eyes wide. 'How come?'

I shrug. 'School number one I went to until I was ten – till Dad left. I loved it there, but we had to move, and that meant school number two. I wasn't very happy back then – surprise surprise – and I kept getting into scrapes. This one girl said my dad had left because he was sick of me, and we had a fight and I knocked her tooth out.'

'You did?' Holly says, aghast.

'Well, it was only a baby tooth. Probably.' I frown. 'That was the end of school number two.

Mum packed me off to stay with my nan in Milton Keynes – school number three. I only lasted there a term. Nan said I was a hooligan and I needed some firm discipline, and she sent me to stay with my Uncle Jon. That was school number four, my first secondary. I was there for six months, but I got suspended twice.'

'Jeepers,' says Holly.

'Then it was back to London, to Greenhall Academy, which was a nightmare from start to finish. So getting worked up about school number six – well, why bother? It can't be all that long till the summer holidays start, and there's no way I'll be sticking around much longer than that. I mean, it's hardly worth turning up at all.'

I glance at Holly through narrowed eyes to see if she's up for a day's skive, but her jaw drops at the very idea.

'You have to go in,' she protests. 'It's school!'

'Yeah, it's school,' I echo. 'When does that bus come, did you say?'

'Half eight,' Holly says. 'Any minute now.'

'OK.' I grin. 'Look, I've left my pencil case behind. Don't want to be in trouble before I even start – I'll run back for it. Won't be long!'

I turn back down the lane, walking briskly – as briskly as you can on three-inch wedges, anyway. They are out of their tiny minds if they think I

46

am going to school today. Primary school? I'm sorry, it's just *not* happening.

Secondary is bad enough; you spend the day shaking hands with teachers and filling in forms and being shown about by geeky kids keen to get you involved in chess club and maths club and after-school sports. Great. Primary, though, that's a million times worse. Gym class in your knickers, star charts for good behaviour and lunchtime recorder lessons? No thanks.

'Scarlett, wait!' Holly yells after me. 'You'll miss the bus!'

'Maybe,' I call back to her. 'Maybe not. Don't stress, Holly!' I turn the corner, scramble over a bit of tumbledown wall and duck out of sight in the trees. I stand still, listening, and after a few minutes I hear the school bus draw up further along the lane. The engine idles for a few minutes, so I guess Holly has made it wait. Eventually it revs and then fades, and the morning air is still again.

I sit down on a fallen tree trunk and text Mum, asking her to relent and let me come home. There's no reply. I eat some crisps left over from yesterday's packed lunch and play Snake for a while on my mobile, surprised at how calm and peaceful it feels to be sitting alone in the dappled green light of the woods.

I'm sleepy now, which isn't surprising because I

haven't slept properly for days. I could curl up on the forest floor in a nest of leaves and bracken, or I could sneak back to Dad's, slide under that patchwork quilt and sleep the day away in comfort. I venture out of the woods and clunk back down the lane to the cottage. With any luck, Clare will be busy mixing up cauldrons of soap in the workshop and Dad will be plugged into his PC doing webby stuff, and I'll be able to sneak upstairs unnoticed.

Fat chance. The front door squeaks as I slip inside, and I get no further than the third step before Dad's voice says quietly, 'Scarlett? What exactly is going on?'

I try the line about forgetting my pencil case, but Dad isn't fooled. His lips set into a thin line, so I smile my infuriating smile, just to wind him up a little more.

'I'll take you myself,' he says grimly. 'I should never have trusted you to go on the bus.'

'I don't feel well,' I protest. I really don't, not just because I'm tired, but because my tummy is doing backflips with the crisps and the muesli, and the ache in my chest from yesterday is back. It's probably a virus, or a rare kind of allergy – to school.

Dad doesn't care. The Morris Traveller rattles through the lanes, Dad gripping the wheel in stony silence as he delivers me to my fate. He keeps it up for a whole five minutes before caving in.

'OK, Scarlett,' he says, his face creased and frowny. 'I know your mum went back to her maiden name after we split up, and she told me you were using the name Murray too. Actually, though, you're still legally Scarlett Flynn. I thought it'd be easier if I enrolled you at Kilimoor as that. OK?'

No, Dad, that's not OK. I don't want your name. I don't want to be part of your poxy new family.

'Whatever.' I shrug.

Joining a new class mid-term is not easy, despite what I said to Holly. It takes guts to walk into a place you've never been and act like you couldn't care less. People know you've got a story, and they're hoping it's a juicy one. They can't wait to weasel it out of you. A broken home? Cool. Excluded from your last school? Wicked. Weirdo, freak, loser? Tell me about it.

I'm used to it now, of course, but you have to be cool, you have to be calm, you have to play it right. You have to make an entrance.

That's what I do, all right. Dad drives right into the playground and screeches to a halt just as the bell for break peals out.

Kids swarm out of the school towards us, then stop, gawping. I can see Holly, with her mile-wide grin and her shining face. I can see a geeky girl

49

and a lanky, ginger-haired boy, but the other kids seem very young. They are amused by my wedge sandals, my fluffy rucksack. They whisper and point at my ketchup-coloured hair.

I look around the playground for a stone to crawl under.

Dad starts explaining my late arrival to the teacher, Miss Madden, who peers at me over her glasses, looking faintly horrified. She dredges up a smile.

'Miss Flynn,' she says, and I can't help wincing at the name. 'All the way from London, so. Well, I'm sure you'll settle right in.'

I'm sure I won't.

'Yes, Miss,' I say.

The wedge heels don't help – I am head and shoulders taller than every other pupil in this dump. I feel like a lion that's mistakenly wandered into the small furry-animal enclosure at the zoo. I don't fit.

OK, all I have to do is roar loudly and they'll back away, but the more those kids laugh and whisper in their weirdo sing-song accent, the more it feels like I'm the one who's nervous.

Small children can be very, very scary.

Holly appears at my side, brown eyes reproachful. 'Did you really forget your pencil case?' she wants to know.

'Not my pencil case, my flick knife,' I growl, and watch her eyes widen. 'Joke, Holly, OK? I don't carry a flick knife. You shouldn't have made the bus wait, y'know. I'm not worth it.'

'I think you are,' Holly says.

'More fool you.'

The bell rings for class and the geeky, dark-haired girl appears at my side. 'You're Scarlett, aren't you?' she says. 'I'm Ros. I'm in Sixth Class too. Perhaps we can be friends?'

Do I look that desperate? Probably. I trail inside and flop down in the window seat beside her. The lanky, ginger-haired lad in the seat behind drags his desk back a little, in case I have some contagious disease that's passed on by eye contact. Terrific. He has to be the other Sixth Class kid.

I blow him a kiss, which makes him blush beetroot with disgust. Makes me feel better, though.

'Good morning, Scarlett,' Miss Madden says crisply. 'Welcome to Kilimoor. We're a very small school, and that's bound to feel strange after the high school you've just left in London, but I'm sure you'll fit right in!'

'*Fáilte*, Scarlett,' the class chorus. '*Dia duit*, Scarlett!'

I look blank.

'It's Irish,' Ros whispers in my ear. 'They're just saying welcome, and hello.'

'Whatever,' I scowl, and Miss Madden gives me a sour look. Yup, I'm settling in fine.

By lunchtime, I've ploughed through four pages of maths and completed a geography worksheet on rainfall, all without major disaster. Maybe, just maybe, I am going to be able to handle this place. How hard can it be? It's not just a primary school, it's the tiniest primary school in the known universe.

So what if I'm a lion trapped in the small furry-animal enclosure? They're lucky to have me. My roar is returning by the moment.

Ros, Holly and I eat our sandwiches on the grass, next to the playground where the smaller kids are legging it around with footballs and skipping ropes. The lanky, ginger-haired kid comes up and sits down beside us, shooting me black looks.

'This is Matty,' Ros tells me. 'He's in Sixth Class too.'

Matty downs a ham sandwich in just one mouthful, glowering. I wink at him, which makes him blush purple all over again.

'You think you're so cool, don't you?' he huffs.

'Cooler than you?' I laugh. 'Well, yeah, just a bit, Carrot Boy!'

'You're not so tough,' he says. 'You're just a wimpy, city kid.'

Holly looks indignant. 'Scarlett was expelled from her last school for starting a food riot,' she declares proudly. 'She's not wimpy, OK?'

Somehow, having Holly as my cheerleader strikes me as a bit sad.

Matty glares. He roots around in the bottom of his rucksack for a bit, then draws out a small, crumpled, cylindrical package and sets it on the grass. Ros, Holly and I watch in silence as he unwraps the package to reveal a small, wizened cigarette, slightly bent.

'Ewww,' Holly says.

'Think you're tough?' Matty challenges. 'Prove it!'

My heart sinks.

I've been here before – and I didn't like it. When I was staying with Nan, my friend Ria nicked some ciggies from home and the two of us hid in the school toilets, trying them out. It was disgusting – I coughed so much I nearly choked. A passing teacher heard me and we were hauled up in front of the Head. Ria said the ciggies were mine, and that I'd forced her to try them – the Head believed her.

Nan was furious. She packed up my case and put me on the next bus to Oxford, where Uncle Jon met me with a face like thunder. I didn't touch a single ciggy while I was there, but Uncle Jon was always sniffing my breath and checking my fingers in case they were getting yellow. He was still stressing out over all that when I got sprung climbing in the window after an evening in the park with my friends. It was gone eleven, hours past my curfew. I got grounded for a month and went kind of stir-crazy, and one night when I was mad at Uncle Jon for confiscating my CD player,

I chopped my bedroom curtains into little pieces with Aunty Kay's dressmaking shears.

Whadd'ya know, it was back to London, faster than you could say *snip, snip*. Matty wants to know if I'm tough. He has no idea.

'So?' Matty asks now, offering me the crumpled, ancient ciggy.

'Nah, I'm trying to give up.' I shrug.

'You've never smoked in your life,' he says slyly.

I'd like nothing better than to light up that fossilized little ciggy and blow toxic smoke rings right into his pasty face, but he's just not worth the hassle.

'Look,' I sigh, rolling my eyes. 'Ciggies are strictly for losers. Bad breath, yellow fingers – no thanks.'

'Knew it,' Matty smirks. 'You're chicken.'

I don't like being called chicken – especially not by a lanky, carrot-haired saddo who thinks that smoking is the height of cool.

I stick out my tongue at Matty, and his eyes just about pop out on stalks as he spots my stud. I have instant bad-girl status, top quality.

'Wow,' Holly breathes.

'Is that for real?' Matty splutters. 'You're only *twelve*. How did you get a pierced tongue? Didn't your parents go mad?'

'My friend Em's brother works in a tattoo studio,' I explain. 'He did it. Em told him I was sixteen – I don't think he believed it, but he turned a blind eye. My mum went kind of crazy, but it was too late by then.'

'Did it hurt?' Ros wants to know.

'Not much,' I lie.

'Cool,' Matty breathes. 'Way cool.'

My roar is almost back to full strength. Back in class, Miss Madden hands out Gaelic workbooks and asks Ros, Matty and the older kids to work on exercise fifteen.

'You'll be needing the basics, of course, Scarlett,' she says. 'You can work with the little ones.' She throws me a bright, false smile that feels like ice and hands me a worksheet titled '*Clann*'. It is illustrated with drawings of a man, a woman, a girl, a boy and a baby, labelled with weirdo names like *athair, máthair, mac, iníon, leanbh*.

'*Clann* means "family",' Ros whispers in my ear

I open my pencil case, pick out a crayon and scribble across *athair*'s face.

I can't be certain, but I think Miss Madden is going around the room asking people about their families. Perfect. Dad told me she knows all about me. Doesn't she know I don't have one? Has she picked out this worksheet on purpose? I look at her smiling, chirpy face and my fingers itch to slap her.

I'm finding it hard to concentrate on the page. My throat aches, and there's a lurching feeling in the pit of my stomach. I'm not well, seriously. I need to lie down in a darkened room, possibly for the rest of my life.

'Ah . . . Scarlett, *conas atá tú?*' Miss Madden asks.

I have no idea what she is asking. I can barely follow her accent when she's speaking English, let alone Gaelic. I shake my head.

'*Conas atá tú*, Scarlett?' she repeats, teasing me. '*An bhfuil tú go maith?*'

My head aches. I can't make sense of anything she says.

'She says, how are you?' Ros whispers. 'Are you all right? Say something!'

'I'm a bit hot,' I mumble, and a ripple of laughter spreads out around the class. Of course, I was meant to say something in *Irish*.

'*Oscail an fhuinneóg*,' Miss Madden says, smiling. Why can't she leave me alone? She may as well be speaking Cantonese. She grins prettily, nodding towards the window.

'The window,' Ros hisses in my ear. 'She says, if you're hot, open the window!'

I lean across to fiddle with the catch and let the big, metal-framed window swing open. I look out of it longingly, across the little playground, the neat daisy-sprinkled grass where we sat in the sunshine just half an hour ago. Then I drag my eyes back to the classroom.

'*An bhfuil biseach ort?*' Miss Madden says.

Why is everyone looking at me? I lean back in my chair, staring at a fixed point just above the blackboard, wondering why it keeps going out of focus. Something that feels a lot like panic is forming a small, hard knot inside me.

'Miss Flynn?'

I shove my desk so hard it topples over on to the floor. A gasp spreads out across the classroom like a ripple on water, and Miss Madden's eyes look like they might pop.

'What are you doing, Scarlett?' she asks, switching back to English rapidly, but by then there is no going back. I step up on to my chair as the class looks on, gawping. My wedge heels make a clopping sound as I balance on the window sill before ducking through the open window and dropping down on to the grass.

'Where are you going?' Miss Madden calls out as I stride across the grass, tearing the worksheet into shreds as I walk. Ripped paper flutters out behind me like confetti.

'Scarlett Flynn!' she screeches. 'Come back here!'

I reach the gate and turn slightly, my head held high. The sun is warm on my back but there's a slight breeze, and my head feels clearer than it has all day. Miss Madden is hanging out of the window, calling the name of a girl I can barely remember, a girl who no longer exists. Behind her the class have gathered in a pale-faced clump, fascinated. They seem very far away.

I walk out through the open school gates and don't look back.

The trouble with Kilimoor is that there's nowhere to run to. The main street doesn't have one single normal-looking shop, just an alarming egg-yolk yellow pub called Heaney's Bar, which seems to have a post office and greengrocer's attached. There's a sweet shop that sells sherbet lemons and pear drops straight from the jar and a dusty craft shop selling Aran cardigans and harp-printed tea towels.

I fish out my mobile, hold it at arm's length and take a picture of myself cross-eyed, tongue lolling. *Messed up again,* I text Mum. *Coming back 2 London. Scarlett x.*

Not that she'll be bothered. She still hasn't called.

I find a bus stop, count my cash and wait half an hour for a tiny minibus to appear.

'I need to get to Knock Airport, please,' I say to the driver. 'Do you go straight there or will I have to change?'

'Ah, now,' he replies. 'I'm going the other way.'

'To Dublin?' I ask, because I know you can get ferries from there. The driver just laughs.

'No. You're about as far from Dublin as it's possible to be,' he says. 'Now, you could take the bus to Castlebar, and change there for Knock, but the Castlebar bus went an hour ago. And if it's Dublin you're wanting, you'd best take a bus down to Galway and pick up a coach going east. The Galway bus goes from over the road, by Heaney's. You've just missed it.'

My face falls. 'Is there another one?'

'Friday,' shrugs the bus driver. I stand on the pavement and watch him drive away.

I slump into a little cafe that has red-and-white checked tablecloths and order a bottle of pop and a cheese sandwich for later. The woman at the till squints at me suspiciously.

'You're not local,' she says. 'On your holidays? Staying nearby?'

I push three quid across the counter, ignoring the questions. After all, I am on the run.

'Ah, no, pet, you need euros,' the woman says, pushing back my pound coins. 'Didn't you know?'

I panic. Nobody told me the money was different in Ireland. Can you get euros with a cash card? If not, I am in deep trouble. I need a bus ticket, a plane ticket, a way out of this nightmare.

'I'll leave it,' I say. 'I'm not really hungry.'

There's a racket in the street outside, a horribly familiar racket. I duck out of sight behind a potted palm as the Morris Traveller looms past, gasping to a halt across the street. Dad gets out, white-faced, scanning up and down. He starts going in and out of the shops, grimly, one by one. It doesn't take a genius to figure that the word is out about my Great Escape.

I sneak out of the cafe while Dad is looking for clues in a rundown shoeshop filled with fur-trimmed slippers and shamrock-print wellies. *Buy one, get one free*, the sign says. I cut down an alleyway and follow a footpath along the edge of some fields until I'm well clear of the village, climbing higher and higher up into the hills. Without the cash for bus fare, it looks like I'm walking to Dublin. Maybe I can stow away on a ferry back to England?

I walk until my feet hurt, over the crest of the hill and down into the valley, past small blue loughs that shimmer in the afternoon sun. I climb up the far side of the valley, walk on along the ridge, then drop down on the far side, edging my way down the slope. The gorse and bracken gives way to a woodland of silver birch. My stupid shoes slip and slither, and blisters bubble beneath my toes.

I take cover in the trees, wedge heels crunching over dead leaves and broken twigs. I find a path, then the path fizzles out and I'm back to stumbling over tree stumps and fallen branches, squidging through soggy bits, slipping on mossy stones. Twigs stroke my face like scratchy fingers.

The trees thin out and I find myself on the shores of another lough, a long, dark blue stretch of water that glints and shines. Inside the fluffy red rucksack, my mobile erupts into life. I fish it out, snap open the cover.

'Hello?' I say.

'Scarlett! Where the hell are you?'

'Hi, Mum,' I reply. 'Nice to speak to you too.'

'Scarlett, don't get clever with me,' she snaps. 'Your dad's just been on the phone. What d'you think you're playing at?'

I sit down on a tree stump, cradling the phone. 'I'm not playing, Mum,' I tell her. 'I'm coming home.'

'Scarlett, that just isn't on,' Mum says. 'We agreed this was the best solution, and you won't even give it a fair trial!'

We agreed?

'I've sent you six text messages,' I tell her. 'And a picture, today. How come you only reply when Dad calls you?'

'I had an important presentation yesterday, and then dinner with the clients,' Mum says icily. 'I'd have called tonight, obviously.'

'Well, thanks,' I quip. 'It's great you can fit me into your busy schedule.'

I can hear Mum fizzing with anger. 'Actually, Scarlett, I was in the middle of a meeting when your dad called. I could do without having to deal with this kind of stunt on your very first full day in Ireland. You can't just walk out of school!'

'I did,' I point out. 'It'll save them the trouble of expelling me.'

'You're going back,' Mum says.

'I'm coming home,' I reply. 'Please, Mum. I hate it here. Nobody wants me. It's a dump. Don't make me stay.'

'Scarlett, don't be ridiculous. Where are you exactly?' Mum asks. 'Are you still in Kilimoor? Chris is out of his mind with worry. Promise me you'll stay put. Just stay still, wait for Chris. He'll sort things out.'

'Mum?' the word comes out kind of mangled. I close my eyes, press my fist against my mouth.

'Scarlett?' she says shrilly. 'Are you still there? Listen to me. It's time you stopped acting like a kid with a tantrum and started to make the best of things. Just grow up and get on with it.'

I snap the phone shut, run down to the water's edge and throw the mobile in one perfect, curving arc right out into the lough. It glints silver as it breaks the surface with a splash, then sinks without trace.

I turn away, furious, marching along the shore, but within minutes I trip, scrambling over a knot of gnarled tree roots, falling heavily. I've torn one of the ribbon ties on my sandal, and a hot, burning pain shoots through my left ankle. My eyes prickle with tears of anger, but I won't cry. I never cry – not since Dad left, anyhow. It'd be like letting him see how much he hurt me. Crying is for kids. I scream instead, a bloodcurdling yell that startles the birds and shakes the treetops before tailing off to a whimper.

I pull off my wedge heels and fling them away into the trees ahead of me, because they've ripped my feet to shreds and I don't care if I never see them again as long as I live.

I hobble along the shoreline, my black tights all ripped and holed, but I can't put any weight on my twisted ankle and I have to give up. There's a tree up ahead, a little twisty tree with soft green leaves that sits at the head of the lough. A bubble of water trickles through its bony roots, and little flashes of red peep through the leaves as I approach. Scarves and rags are tied into its branches, like ribbons in a little girl's hair. Weird.

I blink. Up in the foliage, one of my red and pink wedge sandals hangs, dangling from a tangled loop of ribbon. I sit down, leaning my back against the trunk, letting the icy water run over my toes, looking out across the lough.

My ankle is hurting like crazy, and now I can see it's swollen too. Perfect. I close my eyes, wondering how I have managed to make such a mess of my life. If it's all about choices, I guess I just pick the wrong ones, time after time after time.

The light is fading, streaking the sky with ice-cream colours – vanilla, strawberry, raspberry ripple. If I'm not careful, I'll be spending the night here, burrowing down into the dry leaves, resting my head on a fallen branch. It doesn't seem like such a bad idea.

If this was a kid's fairy tale, birds and dormice would fetch me magical blankets woven from spider's web silk or velvet moss, because it's getting chilly now. I wouldn't be sitting alone by a deserted lough in the middle of nowhere, hacked off, clueless, hungry, cold. I'd have met wolves and woodcutters, witches and dwarves and handsome princes to make my dreams come true.

Yeah, right. Even the birds and the dormice are staying out of my way.

I wish I didn't feel so alone.

Suddenly, on the edge of my vision where the shoreline curves round towards a distant rocky headland, something is moving. I can't see clearly at first, because of the fading light and the soft pink glow of the sunset, but then my eyes stretch wide with disbelief.

The horse comes out of the sunset, galloping along the edge of the lough like something from a dream. I can hear the thud of its hooves on damp mud, see the water splash out around it. It's a stocky black horse with a flash of white at its forehead, hooves feathered with cream-coloured hair that's damp and crimped from the lough. It slows as it turns from the water's edge and comes towards me, shaking its head and blowing hot air through flaring nostrils.

The rider looks down at me, his dark eyes shining, black hair flopping across his face. His T-shirt is faded and worn, his jeans are frayed and one brown hand is twisted into the horse's mane.

'I've been looking for you,' he says.

Of course, a boy from the lough could look right into my soul and turn it inside out. He wouldn't need to ask questions. He'd just pull me up beside him on the big black horse and we'd gallop into the water, splashing through the shallows and out towards the silver-pink horizon.

That doesn't happen. When he says 'I've been looking for you,' I snarl right back with 'Yeah? Well, looks like you've found me now.' He raises one eyebrow, just a fraction, and I cover my mouth with my hands so that nothing else mean and spiky can leak out.

'You're the English girl,' the boy says. 'Half of Kilimoor is talking about you. Figured you'd be halfway to the airport by now.'

I shrug. 'I'm heading for Dublin.'

'So,' he says. 'You're going in the wrong direction.'

The black horse wheels around a little, scuffing up the mud. 'You must have walked six or seven miles over the hills,' the boy tells me. 'You're on Lough Choill, not far from your dad's place.'

'No way!' My cheeks burn until I guess they're about as red as my hair.

'Did you hurt yourself?' he asks, looking at my swollen ankle. 'What happened to your shoes?'

'Lost them.'

The corners of his mouth twitch into a smile. 'Don't tell me, red stilettos?' he asks.

'Funny. Red wedge heels, actually, with ribbon ties.'

'Ah. Much more sensible, obviously.' His eyes flicker up to the leaves above my head, where one sandal still hangs from a branch, spinning slightly. 'You found the wishing tree then? Most people tie on rags or scarves, not sandals.'

'Wishing tree?' I echo. 'What's that?'

'This tree,' the boy says, wheeling the black horse round in a circle. 'The old hazel that marks the spring, the holy well. The water has healing properties, and people come and tie cloth on to the branches to ask for a wish, a prayer, a favour. It's either very holy or very magical, depending on who you believe!'

'I don't believe any of it,' I say coldly. 'It's rubbish.'

'Sure.' The boy laughs. 'Don't tell me you've never made a wish.'

'Wishes are for losers.'

'No, wishes are for dreamers,' he says. 'My name's Kian, and the horse is Midnight. I'm guessing you're Scarlett, right?'

'Maybe,' I reply carelessly.

'Red hair, fluffy bag, a scowl that could turn milk sour.' Kian considers. 'Yeah, you're Scarlett. Want a lift back to your dad's?'

I look at him carefully. He can't be much older than me – thirteen, fourteen at most. His eyes are darker than the lough, his grin is wide and lazy, and his accent dips softly like a whispered song. I love the sound of his name – Kee-an, soft and lilting. There's something strong about him, something cool. He peers at me through a tangle of black, jaw-length hair.

'So. You wanting a lift or not?'

'Not back to Dad's,' I say. 'How about Dublin?'

He looks back at me steadily, his lips twitching into a smile. 'You're joking, right?'

'Do I look like I'm joking?'

I get to my feet, trying for a don't-care attitude, but my ankle gives way and I grab on to Midnight's bridle for support. I breathe in sweet hay and the thick, warm, treacly smell of horse, and somehow it reminds me of a little girl with big dreams and a shedload of wishes that didn't come true. Midnight pushes his nose against my neck, nuzzling gently. It tickles.

'Don't think you're running far on that ankle,' Kian says. 'Better get it X-rayed.'

He wheels the horse round and I look for a saddle to grab on to, but there isn't one. Instead, he leans over and hauls me up in front of him like a sack of potatoes, and I wriggle and yelp and fold one leg over until I'm facing forward. It's way higher up than I imagined.

Midnight sways dangerously beneath me, moving off along the path. 'I don't like this,' I say.

'You'll be fine,' Kian says. 'We'll go slowly. Relax.'

'Dublin then?' I ask hopefully.

Kian laughs. 'I don't think so – not with that ankle, and half the countryside out looking for you. Another time, OK?'

'Yeah, right,' I huff. The truth is, though, I don't even know where I'm running to any more.

I take a deep breath in. Kian wraps his arms round me and buries his fingers in the horse's mane, and I see that his wrists are threaded with bracelets made of plaited leather, braided cotton, beads. We turn away from the twilit lough at a slow walk.

Midnight knows the forest paths, picking his way through the undergrowth while twiggy trees ruffle my hair and clutch at my legs. By the time we've pushed out through the trees and into the tiny lane, I'm leaning back against Kian, relaxed enough to let go of the tight knot of hurt that's been eating at my guts for days. The sound of Midnight's hooves on the road is like a heartbeat.

'Your dad's cottage is just along the way,' Kian says into my ear.

All that walking, and I just found my way back here.

'Not Dublin?' I ask Kian.

'Not tonight, Scarlett.'

When we get to the cottage, the dream is shattered. A weird kind of police car is parked outside in place of the Morris Traveller.

'Is that the police?' I gulp.

'The Gardaí,' Kian whispers. 'The Irish version. I told you your family were worried. No need to mention me, OK? Let them think you made your own way back. I'll see you around.'

'Will you?' I ask.

'Sure I will.'

As I slip down from Midnight's back, he reaches out and touches my hair, so softly, so quickly, I wonder if I imagined it. Then he wheels Midnight round in the lane and heads into the shadows. As I push open the gate, the door opens and Holly runs down the path and into my arms.

'Scarlett!' she squeals. 'I thought I heard something! We were so worried, we thought you'd run away forever and ever.'

'Well, I haven't,' I mutter. 'Obviously.'

'Oh, Scarlett, I'm *so* glad you're back!' She clings on to me so tightly I can barely breathe, which is kind of annoying, but not as bad as you'd imagine. It's nice to feel wanted.

'Scarlett, thank goodness,' Clare says, smiling from the doorway, and Holly drags me forward, towards the bright hallway. When I look over my shoulder, Kian and Midnight are gone, and there's nothing but the quiet clack-clack of hooves on the lane, fading into the distance.

Once the Gardaí have gone, we are left alone in the cottage kitchen, Clare, Holly and me. Dad has been driving around the lanes in the Morris Traveller, looking for me, but Clare called him on his mobile to tell him I was safe and he's on his way back now, so I guess I have yet another round of questions to look forward to.

'Better call your mum too,' Clare says. 'She's been worried sick.'

'Scared I'd turn up in London again, more like,' I huff.

'Scarlett, don't,' says Clare, dialling the number, her face all sad and anxious. She offers the phone to me, but Mum is the very last person I want to speak to right now. It's far more entertaining to watch Clare tackle the woman who's hated her so much, for so long.

'Sara?' she begins, clearing her throat and twiddling her hair with one nervous hand. 'Yes, she's turned up, quite safe. She walked from Kilimoor, over the hills and along the lough. She was heading here all the time!'

Well, not exactly. I planned to walk to Knock or Dublin, or else gallop across the lough to a magical land where nobody is ever sad or lonely. If Clare wants to think I was heading for home, though, that's fine. Why should I care?

'Yes, we'll talk to the school in the morning. I'm sure they'll understand. It's a big upheaval for her, Sara, but she'll be fine, don't worry. She's too tired to speak just now . . . I'll get her to call you tomorrow. Bye, Sara.'

Just then there's a noise like a tractor dragging a couple of dozen old tin cans in the driveway outside.

'There's Chris,' Clare says. 'Thank goodness. I'll run you a bath, Scarlett, then we'll get some dinner on. You'll be starved!'

I manage a weak smile. I know she's just pretending to be kind, like that witch in the fairy tale who fattens up children before she cooks and eats them. I know I shouldn't trust her, but right now I'm too tired to fight back.

'Come on, love,' she says, hustling Holly out of the room. 'Let's give Scarlett some time with her dad.'

I'm alone in the kitchen when Dad comes in, and when I see his face, there's a little stab of pleasure inside of me. You see, running away wasn't just about shaking the dust of Kilimoor National School off my red-and-pink wedge heels. It wasn't just about trying to make it back to London, to Mum. Maybe, deep down, all I really wanted was to lash out, hurt Dad the way he's hurt me.

And I've done it.

Last night I had a bath and ate macaroni cheese, and Clare bandaged my ankle and Dad hugged me and told me never to frighten him again like that. Then I went to bed in the little sky-blue room with the nursery border and slept for the first time in a week, dreaming of the woods and the lough and a boy called Kian on a shiny black horse.

Today, though, it's back to normal. Dad is pacing up and down the kitchen, seriously stressy. Clare sits at the table, stitching at some patchwork and trying to keep the peace.

'OK, Scarlett,' says Dad. 'Talk. Let's hear it – how the last, last chance fizzled out before you even gave it a proper try. Do you know how hard it's going to be to get that school to take you back?'

'I'm not going back,' I tell him.

'Oh yes, Scarlett, you are. Don't you see how much you scared us last night? What happened to the mobile you were carrying?'

'It fell into Lough Choill,' I mutter.

'Your shoes?'

'Can't remember.' I chew my fingernails absently, chipping off a flake of shiny black lacquer.

'Scarlett?' Dad says. 'You have to talk about this, surely you realize that? You can't just expect us to ignore things the way your mother does!'

'She doesn't ignore it, does she?' I fling back at him. 'I wouldn't be here if she did.'

Dad slumps against the kitchen sink. 'Your mum is at the end of her tether, Scarlett,' he says. 'Things were difficult for her after the divorce, and I expect she let you get your own way too much. You started behaving badly and now it's a habit, a habit that's going to ruin your life. Doesn't that mean anything?'

'My life is already ruined,' I tell him. 'You saw to that.'

Dad takes a deep breath in, face creased with guilt. 'Scarlett, your mum and I got divorced. People do,' he says tiredly. 'In the long run it was for the best. We weren't happy, either of us –'

'*I* was happy,' I interrupt, my voice a little shaky. 'Divorce wasn't "for the best" for me. It was the worst, OK? And it's all your fault. So *don't* start telling me how to behave and *don't* start telling me what I can and can't do. You don't have the right,

Dad, OK? You gave up on all that stuff when you walked out on us!'

'Scarlett, enough!' Dad sighs. 'I know you're angry and I know you blame me, but you have to see that you can't go on behaving like this. You need firm boundaries, rules. And as soon as that ankle is better, you're going back to school.'

Yeah, right.

It's lunchtime, and I'm sitting in a cafe with Clare, eating mozzarella wraps and sipping tall glasses of milk. We are in Castlebar, almost an hour's drive from the cottage, because in this crazy, middle-of-nowhere place that's how far you have to go to get to a proper hospital.

I've had my ankle X-rayed, been told there's nothing broken and that I'm a very lucky girl because wedge heels with ribbon ties are the deadliest form of footwear ever invented. Maybe. The new, flat Velcro-strap sandals Clare just bought me in a hiking shop down the street have got to be the ugliest, that's for sure. Sadly, there wasn't a whole lot of choice – I needed something that would fit over my hospital bandage, end of story.

'Good food,' Clare says, polishing off her wrap and hoovering up what's left of the salad and crisps. 'Shall we have pudding? Your dad won't be expecting us back for ages . . .' The waitress wanders over and Clare orders strawberries and cream while I opt for chocolate cake.

'I'm mad about strawberries, with this pregnancy,' Clare says. 'It's a real craving . . .'

I roll my eyes and start fiddling with the menu because I really *don't* want to hear about Clare's pregnancy. It's the final betrayal – proof that Dad has moved on. He's got everything he wants now – a country cottage, a stay-at-home wife, a cute little girl with her hair in bunches and a new baby on the way.

Then, guess what, I turn up on the doorstep like a redirected parcel and everything goes sour.

Clare takes the menu out of my hands. 'This must be hard for you,' she says. 'I can see that you might be feeling angry, lost. Please give us a chance, though – we really want this to work.'

And I really *don't*.

'What actually happened at school, Scarlett? What made you lose the plot?'

I blink. It's such a simple question really, but one that Dad never thought of asking. I take a bite of chocolate cake, but it's too dry, too rich. It sticks in my throat, along with Clare's question.

'Dad enrolled me as Scarlett Flynn,' I say at last. 'I'm not Scarlett Flynn any more, OK?'

'OK,' Clare says. 'You can be Scarlett Murray. That's fine.'

'I'm not Scarlett Murray either. Just Scarlett.'

Clare nods her head, frowning slightly. 'Just Scarlett. OK.'

The ache in the pit of my stomach is back, and that choking feeling in my throat. 'I don't feel well,' I say to Clare. 'I haven't for a while. I felt bad on Thursday, at school, and it just got worse as the day went on.'

Clare narrows her eyes. 'OK. So – you were feeling, what, sick? Headachey? Feverish?'

I nod, because I felt all of those things, and that was just the start. 'It got worse when Miss Madden started up with that Irish stuff. I had sort of an ache, here –' I press a fist against my chest – 'and here, in my throat, so I could hardly speak. My heart was thumping too. Do you think it's serious?'

'Could be a panic attack.' Clare bites her lip. 'What were you doing, in Irish? What was the work?'

'Some worksheet,' I mumble.

'Was there a theme?'

'The family,' I whisper.

She puts an arm round me, and I want nothing more than to burrow into her soft, warm body and cry until the hurt goes away. I can't, though, because if I did that, there'd be no going back. Instead, I shake her arm off my shoulder, roughly. 'Don't!' I growl. 'Just don't, OK?'

I feel the anger rising like a tidal wave, flooding my body and making my hands shake. I slam out of the cafe, and even though I'm limping a little I'm halfway down the street before Clare catches up with me. She grabs on to my sleeve, pulls me round to face her.

'Scarlett,' she says. 'Scarlett. It's OK!'

I shake her off but she grabs me again, hanging on this time. 'Count to ten,' she says softly. 'Then take some nice, steady yoga breaths and let the anger go.'

'Leave me *alone!*' I scream, and the cry seems to split the air around us. 'Leave me alone,' I repeat, my voice no more than a whisper now.

'I can't,' Clare says calmly. 'I won't, Scarlett. I'm here, OK?'

'I don't want you,' I choke out.

'I know, and I'm sorry,' Clare says. 'But I'm here all the same.'

I turn my head away and fight to keep back the tears because I don't want her sympathy and I don't want her help. She's the enemy, and I can't let myself forget that.

Not now – not ever.

There's a sound like hail against the little window of the sky-blue room with the nursery border. Then again, I may have imagined it, because you imagine all kinds of stuff, lying alone in the dark trying to keep the bad thoughts at bay.

The room is silent, apart from the gentle swoosh of the swing tree, rustling in the breeze, and some sheep in the field beyond the garden. I snuggle back into my pillow.

Then I hear it again, and I'm sitting bolt upright, my heart thumping. I slide out of bed, edge across to the window and peer out from behind the curtains. And there it is again, a shower of gravel flung up against the window from the garden below, making me jump, making me laugh.

A boy with black hair is standing in the moonlit garden, grinning up at me, arms folded. Behind him, in the shadows at the foot of the garden, I can see a large, dark shape browsing through the flower beds, crunching the blooms from Clare's roses. Midnight. I *like* that horse.

I unlatch the little window and lean out into the night. 'Kian!' I whisper. 'What are you *doing*?'

'Keep your voice down,' he hisses. 'C'mon! Quick!'

I shut the window and dress quickly, heart racing. The cottage is silent, sleeping, as I creep down the stairs. Nobody turns a light on or calls out. I pocket an apple from the fruit bowl, pull back the latch on the back door and slip out into the darkness.

Kian is sitting on the tyre swing, swaying slightly. A stalk of mint from Clare's herb garden dangles from his smiling mouth.

'Hi,' I whisper.

'Hi,' he says, nodding at my bandaged foot and saddo sandals. 'Like the footwear.'

'Mmm. Super cool.'

Midnight appears behind me, snuffling at my pocket for the apple. He sniffs, draws back his lips and crunches into the fruit with huge, yellow teeth. His nose is unbelievably soft, like warm velvet.

'He likes you,' Kian says.

'He likes apples,' I correct him. 'But hey, I'm not proud!'

Kian vaults up on to Midnight's back, pulling me up beside him. I'm so close I can smell the mint on his breath. Down at the end of the garden,

Midnight picks his way carefully over a bit of tumbledown wall, half-hidden behind Clare's workshop. We ride out across the field, down towards the woods and the lough.

'So,' says Kian into my ear. 'Everything OK, the other night? No hassle from the Gardaí?'

I shake my head. 'They didn't quiz me about strange boys on horseback, if that's what you're asking.'

'Good,' Kian says as we enter the woods, dark silhouettes of trees closing round us. 'I don't get mixed up with them unless I can help it. How about the ankle?'

'It's not broken, just badly twisted,' I say. 'The doctor kept going on about wedge-heel sandals, but I blame the tree roots.'

'Obviously.'

'All the same, next time I run away, I'll plan my footwear better.'

'Running away's overrated,' Kian says. 'You just drag your troubles right along with you.'

'Yeah, well, I've got plenty of them,' I grumble.

'You could always stick around,' Kian says softly. 'It's not so bad. This is my favourite place in the world – kind of timeless, magical.'

I grew up in London, with grey pavements and neon skies and litter. The only magic I ever saw there was when someone decorated the bus shelter outside our house one night, with spray-can graffiti in a dozen different colours. 'That's not magic,' Mum had sniffed. 'It's vandalism.'

Midnight moves slowly along the dark woodland path, hooves crunching over leaves and twigs. Suddenly, an owl swoops past us, ghostly pale, the breeze from its wings cool against my cheeks. I'm grinning in the dark, I realize, eyes wide.

'See what I mean?' Kian whispers.

We come out of the woods right by the hazel tree at the tip of the lough. Kian dismounts and I slither down beside him in the moonlight. Midnight drifts off, cropping grass, and I sit down beneath the hazel tree. Kian flops beside me, just a breath away. A crescent moon hangs silently above us, painting the world with silver.

'I can see why you like it,' I admit. 'I guess I'm just not a country girl. Maybe I'll get to like it too!'

Right here, right now, I feel safer, calmer than I have in a while. I'm not sure it has anything to do with the woods and the lough, though. Maybe more to do with a skinny boy with dark eyes, raggedy black hair and slanting cheekbones.

'Stick around, Scarlett,' he says again.

'Don't know where else I can go,' I admit. 'I was aiming for London, the other night, but Mum doesn't want me there. Nobody wants me here either, not really. Maybe Holly, but then she's nuts to start with.'

'Who's Holly?' Kian asks.

'My stepsister,' I explain, trying out the feel of the word in my mouth. It's weird, alien, like the piercing when I first got it. Like the piercing, I guess I'll get used to it.

'So – happy families, right?' he says. 'Think you'll settle in?'

'They don't need me,' I tell him. 'Dad's moved on, got his new wife, new daughter, new baby on the way. What do they want me for?'

'No idea,' Kian grins. 'Can't see the attraction, myself. Bad-tempered, skinny kid with ketchup hair and poor taste in footwear . . .'

'Hey!' I protest. 'I have *great* taste in footwear!'

He raises one eyebrow, his gaze flickering over the scary Velcro walking sandals. 'Sure you do,' he laughs.

I know he's teasing me, but I want to be cool, I want to be wild. I want to be a million miles away from a nice family girl in sensible shoes. I want Kian to know that.

I let the gold stud click against my teeth, so that he sees it. He doesn't look disgusted, like Mum when she first saw it, or horrified, like Miss Phipps. He isn't shocked or impressed, like Holly, Ros and Matty. He just looks curious, maybe a little sad.

I wish I'd kept my mouth closed.

'OK,' he says. 'Why d'you do that?'

'Don't know.' I shrug. 'It seemed like a good idea at the time.'

Like about a million other good ideas I've lived to regret. What are you meant to do when you're crying inside and nobody even notices? You can shout and swear and stamp your feet, get into trouble at school, dye your hair paintbox-red. You can stay out late, skip school, tell lies, break things. You can even pierce a hole through your tongue and scare old ladies on the bus, but don't expect anyone to see what's happening inside. They never will.

'Whoever you were trying to shock, I hope it worked,' Kian says.

'Fat chance,' I reply.

There's a silence, and I flop back on the grass, watching the ink-black sky through the branches of the wishing tree. Kian is beside me, a whisper away through the rustle of long grass.

'It'll be OK,' he says into the dark, so softly he could almost be talking to himself. 'Everything'll be OK.'

I close my eyes, shutting out velvet skies and silver stars and wizened hazel branches silhouetted against the moon like gnarled fingers. The ground is cool, the grass soft, and I can hear Midnight chewing grass and Kian breathing and the sound of the lough sighing gently against the shore. It feels like home.

When I wake, the sky is lighter, streaked with apricot and peach. Kian is shifting too, stretching and yawning, and Midnight stands a little way off along the loughside, drinking, swishing his tail, making little huffing noises through his nostrils.

'It's daylight!' I panic. 'I have to get back. If they think I've run off again, they'll just about kill me.'

'OK. No problem.'

Kian whistles softly and Midnight lifts his head, shakes his mane and strolls lazily towards us, round belly swaying.

The woods are waking up, birds singing in the trees, red squirrels darting through the branches. The light is cool and dappled green, and there's a sharp, fresh smell of morning. We ride through the woods and come out into the lane, just a little way from the cottage.

'It's early,' Kian says as I slip down from Midnight's back. 'Well before six. They won't be awake.'

'Did we really stay out all night?' I ask, amazed.

'Not *all* night. I didn't call for you till after twelve.'

'You're a bad influence,' I tell him. 'Dad wouldn't approve.'

'How about you? Do you approve?' He reaches down from Midnight's back and drops a kiss right on the tip of my nose, so light, so quick, it's no more than a little breath of air.

'Did I dream you?' I ask him as he wheels Midnight round in the lane. 'Seriously. Are you sure you're real?'

Kian laughs. 'I'm not sure of anything,' he says, turning down the lane, back straight, shoulders level, tanned fingers knotted into Midnight's tangled mane. He looks back over his shoulder, grinning. 'So long, Scarlett. Dream on.'

I creep under the covers at dawn, feeling warm and shivery and full of hope. I can't stop smiling because I've never known a boy like Kian before, a boy who makes me feel safe and special, a boy who wants me to stick around.

I don't know much about him. I don't know his surname, his age, his address or phone number. I don't know the name of his favourite band, his hopes, his dreams, his likes, dislikes. I don't know if any of this matters.

I'm falling for him anyway.

I know Kian is a bad-news boy – anybody who calls for you at midnight with a handful of gravel is unlikely to be a boy scout. Mum and Dad and Clare would not approve, but then, I don't approve of them either, so what does it matter?

I close my eyes, and my head fills with pictures of a black-haired boy with sunbrown skin, a boy who laughs easily, talks softly. I can see the sunrise painting the water silver, see a big, black horse wading out into the water to drink. It happened, and it was magic, it was mine.

I can hear people moving about downstairs, laughing, talking. Sunshine peers through the crack in my curtains, warming my face and arms, and there's a gorgeous cooked-breakfast smell in the air.

I rub my eyes.

'Scarlett, breakfast's ready!' Dad shouts up. 'Don't let it go cold!'

I roll over, burrowing down beneath the quilt. I don't do family breakfasts, especially not with this patched-up excuse for a family. But isn't it kind of a waste of sunshine to lie in bed all day?

I wash quickly, drag on some clothes and hobble downstairs. In the kitchen, Dad is frying eggy bread like he used to do when I was little, and Clare is dishing out baked beans, grilled mushrooms, tomatoes, fried onions, potato cakes. There's not a sausage or a bit of bacon in sight, and my mouth twitches into a smile before I can hide it. It's a vegetarian brunch, and it looks fantastic.

'We're eating outside,' Clare says. 'Go on and sit down.'

I mooch out into the garden, where Holly is setting the table with a red spotted cloth and pouring orange juice into glasses. I look around for evidence of Kian and Midnight, but there's nothing. It's like last night never happened.

Dad and Clare come out, carrying mismatched china plates laden with food.

'French toast!' Holly exclaims. 'Yum!'

'Eggy bread, we used to call it,' Dad says, trying to catch my eye. 'It was your favourite, Scarlett, remember?'

'Think you're mixing me up with someone else,' I say coldly. Does he think he can buy me with a cooked breakfast and a shared memory?

'Well, it's definitely *my* favourite,' Holly says chirpily. 'From now on, anyhow. I think I might go vegetarian, like Scarlett. I wouldn't miss meat, except for sausages, and you can get ones made out of tofu or something, can't you? Do smoky bacon crisps count?'

'Let's not do anything hasty.' Dad frowns.

'Why not?' I chip in, just to bug him. 'If Holly wants to give up, I'd say the sooner the better. The average person eats over a thousand chickens, twenty-three lambs, eighteen pigs and four cows in a lifetime. Think of the lives you'd be saving, Holly!'

'Right,' says Holly, looking slightly alarmed. 'And do crisps count, did you say?'

'Absolutely,' I say with conviction. 'Everything

counts.' I spot a couple of chickens scratching about under the table for scraps. 'Why would anyone want to eat these little guys?'

'I don't,' Holly decides. 'I won't. I'm going to do it – go veggie. Will you help me?'

'Of course I will,' I tell her, and I'm rewarded with the kind of bright-eyed, adoring look I've only ever seen on spaniels before. 'It'll be cool – you won't regret it, Holly.' But Dad and Clare will, and that, of course, is half the fun.

Dad scoffs the last of the eggy bread, eating it spread with strawberry jam, the way we used to.

'Jam?' says Clare. 'Disgusting.'

'You'd be surprised.' Dad grins, winking at me.

Holly rinses the empty jam jar with the garden hose, and wafts around the garden picking flowers to arrange in it. She has some seriously sad habits. 'Mum,' she calls up from the end of the garden. 'Something funny's happened to the flower bed!'

Everybody wanders down to take a look. The flower bed is full of crater-like holes where Midnight's hooves sank into the soft soil last night, and the flowers are either eaten or trampled. It looks like a small herd of elephants has been to visit.

'What on earth . . .?' Dad exclaims, baffled.

I could tell them all about the carnage, of course,

but would they believe me? No. Would they blame me? Yes.

'I told you to fix that broken bit of wall down by the workshop,' Clare huffs. 'Something's been in here – cattle, or deer, or something.'

'A horse,' I chip in helpfully.

'Don't be silly, Scarlett,' Dad says. 'There are no horses nearby. It'll be deer.'

'I don't care if it was wolves or wild boar,' Clare grumbles. 'It's ruined my garden. Get that wall fixed, Chris. Today.'

Dad sighs, and I remember that DIY was never his strong point. I think of the pine shelves that he put up in the kitchen in Islington. He huffed and grumbled all afternoon, making me hold the spirit level and find the right Rawlplugs, and after all that Mum still said it was wonky. It didn't look so bad once we'd camouflaged it with pretty plates and dishes, though. And then, at half-past two in the morning, the whole shelf collapsed and every single plate was smashed to pieces. I remember the three of us standing there, in pyjamas, surrounded by broken cups and dishes and serving bowls, laughing till the tears ran down our cheeks.

'Don't worry about it,' Dad says now. 'I'll get it sorted, Clare. It's all dry-stone work, isn't it? How hard can it be?'

He looks at me and catches the glint in my eye. 'Don't, Scarlett,' he whispers. 'Don't say a word.'

And somehow, both of us are smiling.

'Scarlett,' Dad shouts out into the garden, where I am painting Holly's toenails with a glittery green nail polish called Lime Pickle. 'Your mum is on the phone again.'

'Don't want to talk to her.'

It's the sixth time Mum has called since the night of my Great Escape. It's the sixth time I have refused to come to the phone.

'Scarlett, please,' Dad appeals from the kitchen doorway. 'You have to talk to her sometime.'

'Do I?' I ask. 'Why, exactly?'

'She's your mother,' Dad huffs. 'She's worried about you. And besides, she's giving me a really hard time. She thinks I've turned you against her.'

'Nope, she managed that all by herself,' I tell him.

'Go on,' Holly chips in, wiggling her shimmery green toenails in the evening sun. 'You'll hurt her feelings.'

'No chance,' I reply. 'She doesn't have any.'

Dad trudges back inside, defeated. 'Serves her right,' I tell Holly, and she looks at me sadly with those spaniel eyes.

Clare is sitting in a garden chair a few metres away, stitching at a small piece of patchwork, a work in progress. It looks like a cot quilt for the new baby, little scraps of fabric pieced carefully together with bright, decorative stitching over the top. I wonder if my mum ever sat up late stitching patchwork for me? No chance.

'That's cool,' I whisper to Holly. 'The quilt, I mean.'

'It's for the baby,' Holly says. 'It was my idea. It's got bits and pieces from all our favourite things, Chris's old jeans, my dresses, Mum's flowery skirts . . .'

Clare hears us talking and looks up from her sewing. 'The idea is to give a little bit of something we each love to keep the new baby safe and warm,' she explains. She looks at me and her eyes light up. 'I don't suppose . . .?'

She looks at me keenly, like she might be about to ask for a slice of my red fluffy rucksack, but I glare at her and she thinks better of it, gathers up her patchwork and heads inside. She's learning.

Holly, by contrast, doesn't know when to shut up. 'Talk to your mum,' she wheedles. 'You can't ignore her forever!'

I frown. 'Look, Holly, my mum doesn't want me. Nor does Dad really, and I know I'm just a nuisance to you and Clare. Don't expect me to start playing happy families, OK? My life's not like that.'

'We *do* want you!' Holly squeaks. 'Mum really likes you, and I've always wanted a sister – sorry, a *step*sister. As for Dad . . .'

A cold silence falls down around us, and my scalp prickles. 'Holly,' I say quietly. 'He's *not* your dad, OK?'

Holly bites her lip, dragging a hand across her eyes, but not in time to stem the tears. She makes a little strangled noise, jumps up and runs inside, tipping the Lime Pickle nail polish over. It makes a little puddle of glittery goo on the grass, then seeps slowly away, and I'm left wondering why it's me who feels like I'm the one to blame.

In honour of Holly's first veggie weekend, Clare makes banana curry with poppadoms and onion bhajis. Holly kicks my foot under the table, giving me a sad, wide-eyed look designed to say sorry. I wink back, relaxing a bit. She didn't mean to upset me.

'Good to see you two girls getting on,' Dad says, snaffling yet another onion bhaji. 'It's been a good weekend.'

'Don't know how I've lived through the excitement,' I say.

'I liked it,' Holly argues. 'This is the weekend I went vegetarian! And we fixed up the wall, we played Cluedo, I got my toenails painted. You even helped me dye my bedsheets orange!'

'Bedsheets?' Dad echoes, looking alarmed, but Clare hushes him. She picks up a bowl of ripe strawberries, fresh from the garden, and sets it on the table along with a dish of thick, yellow cream. Everybody digs in.

'You'll need to talk to your mother sometime, though,' Dad says, biting into a strawberry. 'And to us, come to that. We need to get things sorted, talk to the school, get you settled properly.'

'No,' I say. 'I won't talk to Mum and I won't go back to that school, OK? It's not happening.'

'It's only a fortnight until the end of term,' Clare says lightly. 'Perhaps a fresh start, after the summer?'

Dad wavers for a moment, unsure whether to stick with the tough-dad attitude or grab on to Clare's suggestion. He hates fighting, I remember that much. He's way better at the fun stuff.

'We *do* need to talk, Scarlett,' he appeals.

'Sure,' I say carelessly. 'We'll talk later. Have a strawberry, OK?' I feed him one of the red berries from my dish, to shut him up and sweeten him up, and pretty soon everyone is feeding everyone else ripe strawberries and laughing.

As a diversionary tactic, it lasts a whole thirty seconds.

'Come on, Scarlett, open up!' Dad grins, and like a fool I open my mouth and wait for the soft, ripe strawberry to land on my tongue. It doesn't. Dad just stares, and Holly gulps and when Clare finally looks up to see what's going on she drops her spoon, spattering cream across the tablecloth. I close my mouth pretty sharpish, but by then it's too late.

'Oh, Scarlett,' Clare breathes.

Dad just puts his head in his hands, distraught. You'd think I just bit the heads off a couple of his pet chickens.

'It's just a piercing, Dad,' I say, but my voice sounds kind of thin and wavery. 'It's no big deal.'

'No big deal?' Dad repeats, quietly. 'No big deal? Scarlett, what the *hell* was your mother thinking of?'

'She didn't know about it until later,' I tell him. 'It wasn't her fault.'

'No?' Dad is struggling to keep his voice steady, and his eyes glitter with pain. 'You are twelve years old, Scarlett, and you're acting like you're on a self-destruct mission! Your hair, your clothes, the way you act – now this! What's happened to you, Scarlett?'

'My life's a mess,' I tell him. 'Haven't you noticed?'

'I've noticed,' Dad says. 'And I think maybe your mum is right – we need to find a counsellor, someone who knows how to help troubled teenagers. We need help. *You* need help, Scarlett.'

I stand up, a little unsteadily, and walk slowly out of the kitchen and up the stairs to the sky-blue room with the nursery border. I feel sick. My tongue is heavy and my mouth is filled with a sour, metallic taste. I'd take the gold stud out of my tongue, but that would leave a hole, a wound that might never heal. Besides, I'm kind of used to the sour taste, these days.

I think of Kian, I think of Dad and Clare and Holly, and I pull the gold stud loose and chuck it across the room. It rolls across the rug and disappears down a crack in the floorboards, and I'm glad. I don't care if I never see it again.

There's a creak on the landing and someone knocks. I ignore it, but Clare's face peers round the door.

'Get lost,' I snap, but she doesn't seem to notice. She comes right on in and sits down on the end of my bed.

Stepmothers are not meant to be soft and smiley and pregnant, they are meant to be hook-nosed and spiteful, stirring up trouble and making you sleep in the cinders. Clare can't fool me. I don't want her pity, I don't want her kindness. I don't want her.

Trouble is, what I want isn't top of anybody's wish list right now.

'Scarlett, please,' Clare says, biting her lip. 'We're worried about you – we just want to help.'

I can't answer her. I want to scream, but I'm terrified that all I have left in me is a whimper.

'Count to ten, Scarlett,' Clare says quietly. 'And breathe, OK? Calm down!'

I take a couple of breaths in, but I don't feel calm. I may never feel calm again.

'I'm not crazy!' I say.

'I know that, Scarlett.'

'Do you?'

'Yes, I do.'

'So stop threatening me with counsellors and give me a chance,' I say with a shaky voice. 'Listen to me. Believe in me!'

We sit in silence on the edge of the bed. Whole minutes tick by, and then, finally, Clare speaks.

'I will,' she says. 'I do.'

On Monday afternoon, Dad arrives back from a trip to Westport laden with books, folders and stationery. He dumps them down on to the nearest armchair, while Clare rinses salad leaves and cuts granary bread and cheese for lunch.

'What's this?' I ask.

'Work,' says Dad. 'If you won't go to school, we'll home-school you – for now, at least. I've been looking into it on the Internet.'

I blink. If school is a prison sentence, home-education must be solitary confinement.

'I don't want to be home-educated!' I protest. 'It's bad enough being stuck here in the middle of nowhere, without being holed up in the cottage all day with just you two for company!'

'We have to educate you, it's the law,' Dad says. 'And I'm afraid Miss Madden isn't too keen to have you back after last week.'

'Good, because I'm not going back!' I huff. 'You can forget the home-education thing too. I don't want –'

'What do you want, Scarlett?' Clare asks.

I frown, because what I want is something I can't have. It's long gone. A happy family, a proper home, a bunch of friends, a way of waking up in the morning without feeling like there's a cold, hard stone lodged in my chest in the place where my heart should be.

'Listen,' Dad says. 'Your mum is upset about all this, as you know. She's been looking at boarding schools on the Net, and found a good one, all girls, not too far from here. Is that what you want?'

'No!' I choke out. 'Why are you all trying to get rid of me?'

'We're not, Scarlett,' Clare says softly. 'Your mum is just worried. She wants what's best for you, and Kilimoor National School clearly wasn't it. Won't you give the home-education idea a try?'

Clare looks at me steadily. She's on my side.

'Suppose,' I sigh.

Dad lets out a long breath, and Clare breaks into a smile so wide her whole face shines. 'Good girl, Scarlett,' she says. 'Good girl.'

That's something I haven't heard in a while.

'You need to do maths and English,' Dad says, loading up his plate with bread, cheese and salad. 'They're basic. I've bought books that seem about right for your age, so you can do a page from each every day. Otherwise, study whatever interests you. You'll be working because you want to.'

'What makes you think I want to?'

'You're a clever girl,' Clare says. 'You'll like this way of learning.'

'Think of a project,' Dad suggests. 'Something that covers several subject areas. You can use books and the Net to find your information, and Clare and I can help, of course.'

I munch my bread and cheese. 'I could study anything I wanted to?' I ask. 'The lough? The woods? The hills?'

'Yup,' Dad grins. 'That would be geography, with a bit of science thrown in if you made a study of the trees, plants and animals. There's history too – and all kinds of local legends, of course, like the one about the hazel at the lough . . .'

I think of the wishing tree with its red rags fluttering, and a boy who rode out of the sunset on a horse called Midnight.

'I wouldn't have to be stuck in the cottage the whole time, would I? I could go out?'

'Sure,' Clare says. 'You could draw, write, map, measure, record temperature and rainfall, compare place names in English and Irish . . .'

I chew my lip. No teachers, no classrooms, no uniforms, no rules – it's appealing. I'd still be stuck in the middle of nowhere, but maybe even nowhere can be cool if you know the right people. People like Kian.

'Start with what you are interested in, Scarlett,' Clare says lightly. 'It's up to you.'

I can give the idea a try, or I can mess it up. I can choose to stay prickly, or I can let the anger go. Suddenly, letting it go actually seems like an option, like it's a skin I can step out of, walk away from.

I try for a smile, and Clare grins back. Even Dad is looking hopeful.

'I know,' I say slowly. 'I know what to start with. Home economics. I'll make fairy cakes for when Holly gets back from school!'

'Flour and sugar are in the cupboard, butter's in the fridge, eggs you'll have to hunt around the garden for,' Clare says. 'Make plenty!'

'I will!'

An hour later, I arrange slivers of golden sponge like butterfly wings in the yellow buttercream on top of each little cake. They look cute, and they smell wonderful. Holly's going to love them.

'Learning at home's not so bad, is it?' Dad says.

'It's OK. And term still ends in a fortnight, right?' I ask hopefully.

Dad grins. 'In the school of life, there are no holidays,' he says.

Next morning, I load my fluffy rucksack with apples, fairy cakes, pencils and sketchbook, along with a striped picnic blanket.

'I'm going down to the lough to start my project,' I tell Dad and Clare. 'OK? I'll walk Holly to the bus.'

Dad looks like he is about to argue, but Clare chips in. 'Give her some space,' she says. 'It's what she needs.'

Dad takes a deep breath in. 'Fine,' he says. 'Don't go too far, now, Scarlett. And don't be late.'

I open the door on to freedom.

'Wish I could be home-schooled too,' Holly sighs as we walk along the lane. 'Fairy cakes and drawing all day long. You're so lucky!'

'Nah, it's still school, isn't it?' I argue. 'Boring!'

Unless Kian puts in an appearance, of course. Then things could get a whole lot more interesting.

'I'm bad news,' I tell Holly. 'Wild, weird, unteachable! That's what Miss Madden thinks.'

'No,' Holly corrects me. 'You're cool. I want to be just like you.'

'Yeah, well, you're nuts,' I laugh.

The red-and-white school bus looms up amongst the fuchsia hedges. 'Don't say bad stuff about yourself,' Holly tells me seriously. 'I think you're great.'

'You're not so bad yourself,' I say as she climbs up on to the bus. 'Just don't tell anyone I said so.'

The bus trundles off with Holly waving and pulling tongues from the back seat, and I walk on down the lane, duck into the quiet, green world of the woods and find the path to the lough. I want to stay a while, wrapped in silence, the way the trees and rocks and the ground beneath my feet are wrapped in moss and ivy and soft, green lichen.

I leave the woods and settle down beneath the hazel tree, spreading the striped picnic blanket across the grass. I open my sketchbook and draw a tall foxglove with furry leaves and purple, bell-shaped flowers up and down the stem. When you look inside, the petals are pale and speckled. I need paints or crayons to show it properly, but I make my pencil sketch as accurate as I can.

The sun is warm, and I close my eyes for a moment to soak up the heat. When I open them again, the lough seems dusted with silver. There's a crunch of twigs just behind me, and rough, warm hands slide over my eyes, blotting out the light.

'Guess who?'

My heart does some kind of double backflip. Kian.

'Been watching you for a while,' he says, lifting his hands away and flopping down beside me. I can't help stealing a sneaky glance at him, and end up getting snagged by the blue-black eyes, the raggedy hair.

I let a few strands of ketchup-coloured hair fall across my face, hiding my smile. Midnight is drifting across the grass to my left, flicking his tail about in the sunshine.

'So, you're drawing plants?' Kian asks. 'What for?'

'It's a project I'm doing,' I explain. 'About Lough Choill – the woods and the lough and the hillside and the hazel tree. Not just drawings, but research, history, maps, everything.'

'Nightmare,' Kian says. 'How can you put a place like Lough Choill on paper?'

'I'm going to try,' I tell him. 'Dad and Clare are trying this home-schooling thing. It's got to be better than hanging out with a bunch of little kids, anyhow!'

'Sure, but school is school,' Kian argues, grabbing my hand and dragging me to my feet. 'C'mon, let's cut class! Live dangerously!'

I stuff my sketchbook into my backpack and abandon the striped blanket to scramble up beside Kian on Midnight's back. The big black horse snorts and shakes his head, and then we're off, galloping down the loughside, our hair streaming out behind us, hands woven tightly into Midnight's mane.

It feels like I've never moved so fast, felt so happy. My face is stretched into a grin a mile wide as the air whooshes past, Kian's arms are round me and all the time Midnight pounds along, his mane flying, his hooves thumping the grass, his black coat shining like silk.

By the time we come to a halt a while later, back beside the wishing tree, I feel so strong, so alive, I might as well have just flown to the moon and back.

'That was *amazing*!' I say to Kian. 'Seriously, that was the best, the scariest –'

Kian puts a finger to my lips. 'Knew you'd like it.' He grins. 'But right now, we have to find some shelter. See those clouds on the hills beyond the lough? There's rain coming, and soon!'

'It's sunny!' I argue. 'There's no way . . .'

But when I squint at the distant hills, I see clouds I never even noticed before, trailing a soft grey mist. It rolls down the hillside towards us, blurring the purple-green heather.

'What'll we do?' I panic. 'We're going to get soaked!'

'Hey, it's only rain!' Kian says. 'It's just nature, right? What's the problem?'

We slide down from Midnight's back and Kian grabs up the striped picnic blanket and pulls it round us like a cloak, draping it over our heads. The rain hits then, a wall of grey sliding over us, chasing the light away.

'Crazy!' I protest, shivering. 'How can things change that fast? Is it because of the hills or something?'

'Maybe. Sometimes, you can just smell it in the air. Everything's perfect – then the storm hits.'

'Story of my life,' I say. My hair is dripping and rivulets of rain slide down my face.

Kian looks at me sidelong beneath the dripping blanket. 'Change isn't bad,' he says to me. 'Stuff happens. You have to accept it, adapt.'

'I was happy,' I argue.

'So be happy again.'

'It's not that easy!'

'It *is* that easy.' Kian grins. 'Really – try it!'

I look at Kian, his lips slightly parted, the smell of wild mint on his breath. For one split second, I have the strongest urge to reach over and kiss him, but abruptly he drops the blanket and I'm draped in cold, soggy wool, squealing and yelling and chasing him down to the water's edge, where Midnight is standing. The big black horse looks like he just walked out of the water. His coat gleams, and he raises his face to the storm, breath steaming.

Then the rain cloud slides past and the sun reappears. As if by magic, a perfect slice of rainbow appears on the hillside. You don't get many rainbows in London. I know the science, sure – sunlight and rain create a prism of light, all the colours of the spectrum. It's just that I've never seen one like this before. It arches over the hill, chasing away everything sad and dull and ordinary, making you believe in miracles.

'Wow,' I whisper.

'That's Connemara.' Kian shrugs. 'Sun, rain, rainbows, all in the space of five minutes. Storms and sunshine, darkness and light.'

'It's beautiful,' I whisper.

Kian grins at me. 'It is, of course,' he says.

We are silent for a long while, and somewhere in the silence Kian finds my hand and holds it tight. We huddle at the edge of the lough, eating apples and damp fairy cakes, watching the rainbow fade.

Later, Kian walks me home along the lane, leading
Midnight behind us. He's stuck a sprig of velvet-
green leaves behind my ear, so the whole world
smells fresh and cool and good enough to eat, and
he's picking fuchsia flowers from the hedgerow,
showing me how to suck the sweet juice from their
bell-like centres. 'Fairy food,' he says.

'Yeah, right,' I laugh. 'You don't believe in
fairies!'

'Not the storybook kind, obviously.' Kian grins.
'That's kid's stuff. There's definitely something to
it, though – this is Ireland, after all!'

'You're crazy!'

'Not at all,' Kian says. 'Did you never wonder
where all those stories began? Will I tell you? They
began right here. Long ago, there lived a people
who were tall and bright and brave. They knew so
much about the land and the sky and the sea that
they were just about immortal. Then, one day,
invaders came, a few at first, and then so many

there could be no stopping them. They were ordinary folk, farmers, fishermen, soldiers, and they became the Irish people.'

'What happened to the first lot?' I ask.

'They couldn't leave and they wouldn't fight,' Kian tells me. 'So they decided to live alongside the newcomers, but hidden away, like shadows. It was like two worlds existing alongside each other, one real, one magical. The ordinary people could sense they were there, and sometimes they'd leave offerings, ask for favours, especially at places where the veil between the two worlds was thin. That's what the wishing tree is all about.'

My eyes are wide. 'You're winding me up, right?' I ask. 'You don't really expect me to believe that rubbish? No way!'

Kian laughs. 'Aw, c'mon, everybody's got to believe in a little bit of magic!'

He takes my hand and squeezes it tight, and I think of rainbows, the lough glinting in the moonlight, a dark-velvet sky sprinkled with stars. I think of a boy with tanned skin, raggedy hair, a boy who laughs and takes risks and tells tall stories, and I know that there's more than one kind of magic.

'See you, Scarlett,' Kian whispers, and I slip inside the gate with mint and fuchsia flowers in my hair, a smile as wide as Lough Choill.

Holly is on the tyre swing, her back to me, her hair in bunches flying out behind her. She looks like something out of a TV ad for washing powder, squeaky clean and seriously cute. Then she looks over her shoulder and I see that she's been at my make-up. She has painted her lips black, streaked purple blusher across her freckled cheeks. Scary.

'Hi, Scarlett!' she shouts, waving.

'Hi, Holls!' I look over my shoulder, but there's no sign of Kian or Midnight. They have melted away, disappeared back into the woods.

I wander inside, pulling the mint and the fuchsias from my hair to bunch up like a posy.

Clare is at the sink, rinsing strawberries from the garden. She puts the fruit down to rub her back and I try hard to hate her, dislike her even, but somehow I can't. She turns to me, smiling, cradling her tummy beneath the apron, and I hand her the mint and fuchsia posy.

'Lovely!' she says. 'Wild mint. I wonder what that'd be like with the strawberries? Did you have a good day then?'

'Good day,' I tell her. 'Great day, Clare.'

And then I do something neither of us expects. I hug her quickly, shyly, because she may be my wicked stepmother but she cares about me, I know she does.

She has been infuriatingly kind and patient. She

has let me shout and sulk and rage and tried her best to understand. I'm the stepdaughter from hell, pitched up out of the blue to mess up her quiet little life. I guess I am the last thing she needs right now, jumping out of windows, running away, turning her goody-two-shoes kid into a black-lipsticked mini-me. The funny thing is that in spite of everything, Clare makes me feel like she's glad I'm around.

As I pull away, I see that her blue eyes are misty with tears. 'Oh, Scarlett,' she says. 'That's great. I'm so glad.'

'Did I miss something?' Dad asks, mooching through from his study. 'Scarlett? What happened?'

'Nothing happened, Dad,' I say, and watch his face come to life because it's the first time I've called him Dad out loud in almost three years. I fling my arms round him and he holds me tight, and he smells of Polo mints and apple shampoo, just like he always did, and I can't believe how much I've missed that smell. How much I've missed him.

Clare laughs and takes a jug of home-made lemonade out of the fridge, and Dad calls Holly in and the four of us sit round the table, drinking lemonade and eating strawberries tossed in crushed mint and brown sugar.

'Wow,' Dad says. 'Strawberries and mint. I never tried it before.'

'Smells good too,' I chip in. 'You should make it into a soap. It'd be really summery, and you could package it with fresh mint leaves . . .'

Clare's eyes widen. 'You could be on to something.' She grins. 'I'll play around with that idea tomorrow. Thanks, Scarlett!'

I shrug, but hey, it's good to feel like I've done something right for a change. It's good to feel part of things.

I live here now, in the middle of nowhere, with the three people (three and a half?) I once hated most in the world. It's not so bad. They're not so bad. It's not like I belong, exactly, but it's not such a crazy idea that I *could*. One day – maybe. If I wanted to.

That'd show Mum.

My project folder takes shape. I have painted a
map of Lough Choill, complete with hills, woods,
farmland. I have marked the altitude of the ridges
I climbed the day I walked cross-country from
Kilimoor, mapped in Dad's cottage, the lanes.

I have sketched pages and pages of wildflowers
– ivy, wild strawberry and honeysuckle from the
woods; yellow flag, ragged robin and wild mint
from the loughside. I know their names in Latin,
English and Gaelic.

I have a graph to show the temperature and
rainfall, so I know that this summer is shaping
up for a heatwave, hot and dry. Every day I hang
out by the lough, ploughing through dusty old
library books on the long, sad history of Ireland.
I'm also reading legends of long-gone heroes,
warriors, giants, magical princesses with golden
hair and cheeks the colour of foxgloves. They're
as crazy as any story Kian might tell, and
beautiful too.

'This is wonderful stuff, Scarlett,' Clare says one evening, flicking through my folder.

'More than wonderful,' Dad agrees, his eyes shining with pride. 'See what you can do when you try?'

I shrug and smile and pretend I couldn't care less.

Holly and I are holed up in the sky-blue bedroom. I am writing out an old Irish legend for my project folder, about a wicked stepmother who turns her husband's children into swans and leaves them to flounder around above the Irish Sea for hundreds of years. Holly is making a poster from a bit of white card, sketching out the letters and filling them in with vivid rainbow colours.

It's the first day of the school holidays, and Holly has painted her lips blue with my eye pencil to celebrate. She looks cute but sinister, the kind of Hallowe'en trick-or-treater who'd pelt your window with eggs for handing out the wrong kind of sweets.

'Scary look,' I tell her. 'Clare'll go mad!'

'Nah,' Holly says. 'She likes it that we're friends. Wish I could dye my hair, like you. And pierce my tongue! I will, when I'm older.'

'No way, Holly,' I snap, surprised at myself. 'It's not like having your ears pierced, y'know. It hurts. Like *crazy*.'

'Tell me,' Holly says.

I sigh. 'It started out as a dare. My friends dressed me up and shovelled on the make-up to make me look lots older. Like I said, Em's big brother worked in a tattoo place. He did it.'

'Did it bleed?' Holly asks, eyes wide.

'Buckets,' I tell her. 'Well, a bit. But the pain . . . Oh, it was unreal. My tongue was all swollen and Em tried to give me ice cream to eat to cool it down, but I couldn't eat it. I was sick all over my shoes. It was a nightmare. I really wanted to cry, Holly, it hurt that much, but I never cry, no matter what.'

'I know,' Holly breathes.

'Em took me home on the tube and Mum was furious, but she couldn't say too much because she could see how sick I was. She put me to bed and gave me ice cubes to suck and I had to take three days off school. She kept trying to make me take it out, but there was no way I was going to do that after all I'd been through. I was lucky it didn't get infected.'

'Eeuw,' says Holly. 'Sounds awful.'

'If you want to get something pierced, stick to your ears,' I tell her. 'That's not so bad. Well, not normally! I had a friend in London who did it herself with a darning needle and an ice cube – scary! I was there, and I just about fainted!'

'Seriously?' Holly gawps.

'Seriously. Bad news.'

'Ears are boring,' Holly says. 'If it wasn't a tongue, then maybe I could get a pierced nose or eyebrow . . .'

'Yeah, right!' I laugh. 'You're nine years old, Holly! Nobody'd do that kind of piercing for a nine-year-old.'

'But –'

'No buts,' I tell Holly. 'Don't even *think* about copying me. That whole piercing thing was a big mistake – believe me, it's caused a whole bunch of trouble. The crazy thing is, I don't even miss it!'

I stick out my tongue, and Holly looks so solemn that I cross my eyes and squash my nose up with a finger to make her laugh. Then we're both laughing, tickling each other and rolling around on the patchwork quilt until we're breathless, grinning.

Holly goes back to her poster, a sign for the cottage gate to advertize free-range eggs and fresh veggies to passing tourists.

'So,' I say carelessly as I watch her paint, 'tell me about the other kids in this dump. You know, kids my age.'

'Kids?' Holly echoes. 'There are no kids around here. Only Ros and Matty, in Kilimoor, and you've met them already. It's dead quiet.'

'Well, yeah, I'd gathered that,' I say. 'There must

be others, though. Other boys. I thought I saw a dark-haired boy on a horse, the other day, when I was down by the lough. The horse was big and black with feathery cream feet, and the boy wasn't much older than me . . .'

'A boy on a horse?' Holly frowns. 'Don't know who that could be. Matty has an older brother, Paddy – same ginger hair and freckles, but no horse. Then there's Kevin Fahey. Very shy, smells of cough sweets. He's hoping to be a priest one day.'

Kian has black hair, and his breath smells like the wild mint that grows around the lough. I think of how we squashed together in the rainstorm, under the wishing tree, laughing, shivering, his cool cheek against mine.

'I think this is a different boy,' I say.

'Must be a tourist then.' Holly shrugs. 'Or a city boy staying with family for the summer. Where did you say you saw him?'

'By the lough, the other day,' I say vaguely.

'He could be a traveller!' Holly exclaims. 'You know, an Irish gypsy – they camped up by the lough last year, a whole bunch of them. Five big trailers, top of the range, and a couple of trucks and horseboxes. They had some ponies, and a couple of skinny, scruffy dogs.'

'No,' I tell Holly. 'He can't be, he'd have said.'

Holly raises one eyebrow. 'You've *spoken* to him?'

I flush pink, flopping back on the bed to gaze at the ceiling. 'Maybe just once or twice,' I admit.

'Once or twice?' Holly squeals. 'Scarlett, is this why you're always down at the lough? You've hooked up with some gorgeous traveller lad!'

'You're not going to tell anyone, are you?' I panic.

'Of course not!' Holly scoffs. 'I'm great at keeping secrets!'

'OK,' I say, chewing my lip. 'It's nothing, anyway, Holly. We're just friends, and I don't think he's a gypsy. He's really cool, but . . . Well, I don't really know much about him.'

'So ask,' Holly says. 'What's the problem?'

'No problem,' I argue. 'We just don't talk about stuff like that.'

For the first time ever, this strikes me as slightly weird.

'I know his name – Kian,' I offer.

'Kian? Nope, he's not local,' Holly says. 'I'll ask Ros. She'll know – her family have been in Kilimoor forever.'

I sit up, eyes wide. 'Holly, no,' I whisper. 'Don't tell Ros. Don't tell anyone. What if Dad and Clare found out? They'd think he was trouble. They wouldn't understand.'

'No?' Holly pouts. 'Oh well. Don't stress, Scarlett, my lips are sealed. It's so romantic!'

'You think?' I grin.

'Definitely. I can't wait to meet him.'

I chuck a pillow at her, laughing. 'You are NOT meeting him!' I exclaim. 'No way! Seriously, no way!'

'We'll see,' she laughs.

Holly has a friend from school coming over for the day, so I pack my rucksack with bread and apples, ready for a day at the lough. There's no way I want to see any of those Kilimoor kids again – ever.

Clare looks up from the table, where she is stitching new patches into the quilt. Beside her is a heap of scrap fabric and a roll of red ribbon, partly unfurled, snaking here and there through the rags. A memory flickers across my mind, a good memory.

'What's the ribbon for?' I ask Clare.

'Not sure yet,' she admits. 'It was going cheap and I thought it might come in useful. Maybe I'll use it as an edging?'

'Right,' I say.

Clare studies me, eyes narrowed. 'Unless you want it?' she says. 'You'd be very welcome, Scarlett.'

I try for a couldn't-care-less look, but my grin betrays me, and I scoop up the ribbon, winding it back on to the roll and stuffing it into my backpack. 'Thanks, Clare,' I say.

'No worries,' Clare replies. 'See you later, Scarlett.'

Kian is already at the lough when I get there, like he has been just about every day lately. We never plan ahead, it just seems to work out that way. Today, Kian is standing at the water's edge, brushing Midnight until his black coat shines like silk. I fish the ribbon out of my backpack and unravel it, looping it through my fingers as I walk towards them.

'OK,' Kian says. 'Ribbon? Now I'm scared.'

'It's not for you, idiot,' I tell him.

'The wishing tree?'

'As if!' I snort. 'No, it's just an idea I had, for Midnight. I meant to bring scissors, though . . .'

Kian chucks me the brush and walks over to the wishing tree. He reaches up through the branches, almost disappearing beneath the foliage, and brings down an ancient, bulging rucksack. A blackened tin pan is tied to the strap, and a battered spoon sticks out from one of the pockets. He fishes inside, pulls out a pocket knife and hands it over.

I open the blade and slice the ribbon into manageable lengths, then watch him hide the knife away, lift the rucksack back into the tree.

'What else've you got hidden up there?' I ask

him. 'A toothbrush? A sofa? A fifty-piece dinner service?'

'Stuff.' Kian shrugs, sitting down on a rock at the water's edge. 'A bedroll, supplies, some food and hay for Midnight.'

'OK.'

I take the brush and start working through Midnight's mane, smoothing out the tangles. When I was a kid, I dreamt of having my own pony – it was what I wanted more than anything. I used to imagine plaiting its mane with ribbon – now, at last, I can do it for real. The big black horse leans his face against my shoulder as I thread the thin red ribbon into his mane, weaving it in and out.

'Know what I like so much about you?' Kian asks, watching.

'My wit, my charm, my gorgeous looks?' I quip. 'My skill with a horse brush and a bit of ribbon?'

'Well, naturally.' Kian grins. 'All of that. And the way you don't ask too many questions. You just take me as I am.'

'Weird, secretive boy who keeps all his worldly possessions in a tree? What's to ask questions about?'

'Seriously, though,' Kian says.

'Seriously. If you wanted me to know, you'd tell me, right?'

'Exactly. And I don't – I can't. Not yet.'

Midnight sighs, a huge, shuddering breath. I

weave a dozen red-ribbon plaits into his mane, by which time the horse has just about fallen asleep on my shoulder, leaning heavily against me.

'My turn now?' Kian asks.

'To fall asleep on my shoulder or have your hair braided?'

'Either. I'm not proud.'

I ruffle Midnight's mane and blow softly on to his velvet nose, and the big black horse shakes his head and snorts and looks at me from liquid, long-lashed eyes. I plant a kiss on the white star on his forehead.

'I'm crazy about your horse,' I say lightly to Kian.

'He's crazy about you,' Kian shrugs. 'I'm a big disappointment to him these days – no ribbons, no apples.'

'Shut up!' I laugh, digging him in the ribs as we walk back up to the wishing tree. 'I always wanted a horse, when I was a kid,' I tell him. 'A black one, like Midnight. I was going to convert the garage into a stable. I wished and wished for a pony, but I got a broken home instead. I gave up on wishing.'

'Ah, but that was before you met me and Midnight,' Kian grins. 'We're living proof that wishing didn't give up on you.'

'Yeah?' I reply. 'Everything and everyone else did, that's for sure.'

'Not me,' Kian says, his blue-black eyes looking right inside my soul, making me shiver.

'No, not you.'

We fling ourselves down on to the grass, stretching out in the sun.

'So, what's new?' Kian asks.

'Nothing much. The schools have broken up, and Holly has a friend coming over. I'm hiding out here, staying out of the way!'

'Don't blame you,' he grins. 'I guess things will get busier now – kids off school, day trippers, tourists. This place may be quiet, but it's still in one or two of the tourist guidebooks.'

'Seriously?'

'Seriously. We'd better make the most of it.'

Suddenly, away in the distance, there's a squeal of laughter and a crunching of twigs. We jump to our feet. Through the trees, I glimpse two bright figures weaving along, laughing, carrying a picnic basket.

'No way,' I breathe, furious. 'It's Holly – and some kid from the school. I told her to stay away!'

'Too bad she didn't listen,' Kian says.

'I'll get rid of her!' I promise.

I run into the woods, and Holly sees me and waves, crashing through the undergrowth. My anger flares when I see that Holly's 'friend' is Ros, the dark-haired, geeky girl from the school.

'Scarlett!' Holly exclaims, her face all smiles. 'I knew we'd find you! I was telling Ros, you spend all your time down here these days.'

'I *told* you I wanted to be left alone!' I say through gritted teeth.

Holly laughs. 'I know,' she says. 'But you don't mind now we're here, do you? I asked Ros over specially, to surprise you!'

Surprise me? That's not the word that springs to mind. Ros has the grace to blush, but she can't get a word in edgeways.

'We've brought a picnic,' Holly blunders on. 'And we're just dying to meet your friend Kian . . .'

Before I can stop her, she steps out of the trees on to the grass beside the lough, scanning around her. 'Oh. You're on your own. I thought . . .'

Ros and I step into the clearing too. My mouth falls open and a prickle runs down my spine. There is no sign of Kian, no sign of Midnight, even though they were here, right here, just a minute ago.

They may as well have vanished into thin air.

'I thought you said you were meeting him by the lough?' Holly sulks.

'Yup, I said that,' I admit through gritted teeth. 'I also asked you to stay away, didn't I?'

Holly rolls her eyes. 'Aw, you just wanted to keep Kian to yourself. But he stood you up, so it doesn't really matter, does it?'

'He did not!' I blaze. 'He was here, OK? And he'd still be here if you two losers hadn't barged in on things, so thanks a bunch!'

'Stressy!' Holly laughs, but Ros looks embarrassed.

'I didn't realize,' she tells me, tugging at Holly's sleeve as though she can't wait to get out of here. 'Really. I'm sorry.'

'You should be,' I huff. 'We talked about this, Holly – you promised you'd stay away from the lough!'

'Well, I didn't promise exactly . . .' Holly says with a wicked grin.

I remember what Clare said about taking a deep breath and counting to ten. It's a little late for that now, but I try it anyway.

By the time I reach ten, Ros and Holly are turning back towards the woods. 'I thought you'd be pleased,' Holly says over her shoulder. She looks a little hurt, and that makes me feel bad. I try to remember that she's only nine. I got things wrong when I was nine, sometimes. And when I was ten, eleven and twelve, come to think of it. I may be getting things wrong right now.

Kian's long gone, anyhow. I take another deep breath and decide on patch-up tactics. 'Wait up,' I call after them. 'I'm sorry I lost my temper. It's not the end of the world, is it? Why don't you stay, now that you're here?'

'Really?' Holly's face lights up, but Ros looks uncertain.

'Really,' I promise. 'It's OK.'

'See?' Holly grins at Ros. 'I told you it'd be fine!'

She starts unpacking the picnic basket. Ros shifts awkwardly from one foot to the other, biting her lip. If she didn't think I was deranged that day at the school, she's bound to now. She looks like she'd rather be anywhere than here. Well, that makes two of us.

'So,' I say as cheerily as I can manage. 'School's finished now?'

'That's right,' she replies. 'The last few weeks really flew past. Matty and I are moving up to secondary school after the holidays – it'll be so big after Kilimoor.'

'Just a bit,' I agree. 'Kilimoor's tiny, not like any school I've ever known. It kind of freaked me out. You all knew each other so well, like a family or something – and I was the outsider.'

Ros looks anxious. 'We didn't mean to make you feel like that,' she says. 'We wanted you to feel welcome, but – well, it was like you didn't want to be there.'

'I didn't,' I admit. 'I might have been a bit prickly.'

'Maybe a bit.' Ros grins.

'Maybe a lot!' Holly pipes up, and the three of us laugh and the awkwardness ebbs away. Holly stands a bottle of Clare's home-made lemonade in the lough, wedged between a couple of rocks, and we flop down on to the grass. There's a Tupperware box of leafy green salad with feta cheese and cherry tomatoes, along with granary bread, boiled eggs, apples and flapjacks. We fall on the feast like we haven't eaten for a week.

Three swans glide soundlessly down from the hillside, long necks extended, to crash-land awkwardly on the lough with much splashing and flapping of big, white wings. They gather themselves together as if slightly embarrassed, folding their unruly wings into cool origami shapes and curling their necks prettily.

'What was that story you were telling me, about the swans?' Holly frowns.

'A wicked witch put some children under a spell,' I remind her. 'Do you think those are real swans, or enchanted ones?'

'Enchanted, definitely,' Holly breathes.

'Honestly, Holly, you'd believe anything!' I scoff.

'Will you be going to the senior school in Westport?' Ros asks me as we watch the swans glide out into the lough. 'I won't know anyone in our year except Matty. I know some of the older kids, but that's not the same, is it?'

'You'll be fine,' I tell her. 'Give it a week and you'll wonder what you were worried about – you'll make tons of new mates.'

'So you'll be going?' Holly says.

'Holly, you know I won't. The minute I set foot in a school, I get myself knee deep in serious trouble. Home-schooling's safer – nobody can expel me!'

'Don't listen, Ros,' Holly says staunchly. 'Scarlett's cool, honest. I want to be just like her, except I'm having a pierced nose instead.'

'You are not,' I argue. 'We've been through all this! Tell her, Ros – it's a bad idea!'

'For sure,' Ros agrees. 'Imagine the hassle when you get a cold! Yuk!'

'I'm going to do it.' Holly grins. 'You'll see.'

'Yeah, right.'

I pick the shell off one of the hard-boiled eggs and flick it away into the grass. I'm sorry I dismissed Ros as a geeky country kid. She's much nicer, much funnier than I remember, and if she thinks I'm mad, bad and dangerous to know, she's hiding it well. I look at her shiny hair, her pale skin and goofy smile. She's the kind of girl I'd have blanked, a month ago. The kind of girl I avoided like the plague because she reminded me of who I used to be.

We could be friends, maybe. These days, I need all the friends I can get.

'What's home-schooling like then?' she asks, biting into a cherry tomato. 'Is it a skive?'

'It's cool,' I tell her. 'I have to do two pages of maths every morning, but I get to study the things I want to as well, like crazy old Irish legends with swans in them. Dad and Clare let me work out here by the lough too – they trust me, I suppose.'

Would they still trust me if they knew I was meeting Kian every chance I got? Probably not.

'Don't you get awful lonely?' Ros asks.

'Not really. It's good to have some time out. And it's not like I don't see anybody . . .'

135

'So. This Kian – is he your boyfriend?' Ros wants to know.

'Kind of.' He's my best friend, anyhow. He makes me laugh, he makes me think, he makes me dream.

'Sorry we spoilt your afternoon, chased him away,' Ros says. 'No wonder you were cross.'

Holly takes a swig of icy-cool lemonade. 'Aw, come on, Scarlett,' she says. 'He wasn't really here, was he? Not really! You just said that to make us feel bad.'

'He was!' I protest. 'He was right here, till I went into the woods to meet you. Honest!'

Holly frowns. 'Nobody could have disappeared that fast,' she says. 'We'd have seen him.'

'I don't know how he did it.' I shrug. 'And I wish he hadn't, but I'm not going to argue about whether he was here or not, OK? He was.'

'Fine,' Holly sniffs. 'It's no big deal. I just wondered if Ros knew him, that's all.'

'I don't know anyone called Kian,' Ros says. 'He must be a visitor, or a blow-in – you know, like you, new to the area. I've not heard of any new families, though, and my dad runs Heaney's Bar in Kilimoor. If someone sneezes ten miles off, he knows about it.'

'I think he's a traveller,' Holly chips in. 'A gypsy. He's got black hair and a horse with feathery feet, hasn't he, Scarlett?'

'That doesn't make him a traveller,' I point out.

'No, but it might explain how he knows the place so well he can disappear practically into thin air,' Holly muses. 'And it might explain why he's so secretive. C'mon, Scarlett, we're not *that* scary – why did he have to leg it the minute he heard us coming?'

I don't have an answer for that. Being tracked down by Holly and Ros is not exactly the highlight of my day, but I'm coping. Kian could have coped too – he'd have made Holly and Ros laugh, told them stories, charmed them with his blue-black eyes. Holly could have had a ride on Midnight, fed him apples from the picnic.

'Maybe he's from Dublin,' Holly muses. 'An orphan, sent here to live with his grandparents. Or a runaway, a fugitive from justice, living wild in the woods, stealing eggs and trapping rabbits to survive . . .'

I bite my lip, because this seems closer to the truth, even though Holly's version of it makes me laugh. 'He's just a boy,' I tell her. 'No big mystery.'

Holly's eyes widen. 'He could be a ghost,' she whispers. 'The spirit of a boy who died back in the famine times, or maybe a tourist who got lost on the hills in winter, thirty or forty years ago.'

'You're nuts!' I laugh.

Holly chucks the last of the granary bread out

on to the lough, and the three swans paddle furiously into the shallows, gobbling it quickly. I scan them for signs of magic, enchantment, but they're just big white birds, greedy, bad-tempered, with snapping beaks and ruffled feathers, hungry, flapping, scrabbling for bread.

Finally, Mum has got the message. I won't speak to her on the phone, so she stops calling and starts writing letters instead.

I've been through this before. After Dad left, thick letters with bright Irish stamps would plop through the letter box. 'Does he think he can win you round with a letter?' Mum would scoff, ripping them into little pieces to drop into the pedal bin. Before long, I was doing it myself. Birthday cards, Christmas cards, letters, all went into the bin, like so much confetti.

Now it's happening all over again.

I sit by the lough with Mum's latest letter. I don't want to hear about private schools or last, last chances and letting people down. Instead, I smooth the paper out, folding it this way and that until I have made a small, perfect, paper boat. I launch it into the water, and a soft breeze catches it, pulling it out into the centre of the lough.

As I turn from the lough, there's the sound of

a car door slamming in the distance, a movement in the trees to my left. This has been happening lately, since the start of the school holidays. Like Kian said, Lough Choill is on the tourist trail for some very keen sightseers. They come to look at the wishing tree, to fish in the lough, to hike across the hills.

When I'm with Kian, we steer Midnight into the woods, silently, or gallop away down the loughside, out of sight. We make ourselves invisible. Today, though, I'm still waiting for Kian to show up, and I won't let the tourists chase me away. I take out my sketchbook and start to draw the little twisty hazel tree. Its branches are fluttering with wisps of rag and ribbon, and you can still see a red-and-pink sandal peeping through the leaves, if you know just where to look.

The men come striding out of the trees, dark-haired and flint-eyed, smoking and frowning, their eyes scanning all around. They look like brothers, with the same tanned, weather-beaten faces, the same lined foreheads, the same sad, unsmiling mouths. One has a moustache, the other a wide-brimmed hat with a red scarf tied round the brim and a feather in it. Both have the glint of gold round their necks and wrists, and flashy rings on almost every finger. They don't look like tourists. Not like any tourists I've ever seen.

I bend my head back to my drawing, and the men march past, as though I'm not even there. They walk right along the loughside, briskly, until they're out of sight.

Hazel, I label my picture. *Coryllus avellana*, in Latin. *Choill*, in Irish. The tree at the holy well.

I open my notebook and write for a while, listing down all the things that Kian has told me about the tree and the spring. According to legend, the wishing tree is a gateway between this world and some ancient, make-believe world where time stands still.

In that world, in my imagination, the women have long hair and trailing dresses made of velvet, and the men look like extras from *Lord of the Rings*, all bows and arrows and galloping ponies and hair that ruffles in the breeze. You might meet a king from under the sea, or a bunch of swans who turned out to be children, only bewitched. Magic still happens in that world, Kian says.

Wish I could believe in all that stuff.

When I look up again, I see that the two men are walking back, more slowly this time, as though they are looking for something. When they draw level with the woods, they walk along through the trees, kicking at the undergrowth as though something is hidden there, waiting to be discovered.

They stop a few metres away, frowning.

'Hello there, missy,' the older one says. 'Fine day we're having.'

I just stare. Missy? *Please.*

'D'you live nearby, perhaps?' he asks. 'You'd be local?'

Their accent is strong, lilting. I nod my head, very slightly.

The younger man, the one with the hat, steps forward, taking a crumpled piece of card from his shirt pocket. 'We're looking for someone,' he says, his voice low and gentle. 'A boy not much older than yourself, dark-haired, skinny. We thought . . . We thought he might be here, at Lough Choill. Have you seen him? Have you seen him at all?'

It's a school photo. A boy who looks a little like Kian is gazing back at me, his hair shorter and flatter, like someone just raked a comb through it. He's wearing a blue school jersey and a white shirt with a stripy tie, slightly askew.

It can't be Kian, though. This boy looks so sad, so lost, his dark eyes are dead, empty. There are dark smudges under his eyes, like he hasn't slept for a month.

'D'you know him, at all?' the younger man repeats. 'Have you seen him?'

My heart thumps in my chest, and my hands tremble as they grip the sketchbook. These men have come to take Kian, and I don't want them to take him. I don't think *Kian* wants to be taken. I look at the two dark-haired men, keeping my smile bright, my voice steady.

'I don't know this boy, no,' I tell them. 'I live just down the lane. I come here every day, and I've never seen him. Sorry.'

I watch the light drain from the man's face, watch his eyes become as dead as the eyes of the boy in the picture. For a moment, I feel bad, but not bad enough to backtrack, change my story.

'I told you he'd not come back here,' the older man says. 'Why would he? Thanks anyway, missy.'

They turn away, walking back towards the trees, the road. Then the younger man stops, takes off his hat and unties the scruffy red scarf from round the brim. He strides over to the wishing tree, ties the scarf on to the highest branch he can reach and stands looking at it for a long moment.

My heart thumps. Has he seen Kian's rucksack, the bedroll, the hay, wedged out of sight in a forked branch? Maybe not. He turns, tips his hat at me and strides off, through the trees and away.

As if I ordered it specially, the midday sun is hot and the sky is a perfect, shimmering blue. I drop back on to the grass and close my eyes, letting myself drift. When I open them again, Kian is at the edge of the lough, leading Midnight along through the shallows.

I look at him, searching for traces of the sad-eyed boy in the photograph, but all I see are slanting cheekbones, unruly hair and eyes that shine, darker than the lough. Was I right to stay silent? And do I tell Kian about the men who were looking for him?

Kian flops down beside me, grinning. There are wisps of hay in his black hair, like he's been sleeping in a barn.

'You took your time,' I tell him. 'Missed the best part of the day!'

'I found myself some work,' he grins. 'Raking hay for an old farmer guy in the next valley, stacking it up into hayricks. Twenty-five euros and as much hay as I want for Midnight. Same again tomorrow.'

'Cool.'

I pack my sketchbook away, bring out an apple for Midnight. The big black horse ambles over, taking the fruit from my hand softly with a nose like velvet. He crunches the apple with his big yellow teeth, and I push a hand through his mane, ruffling the red-ribbon braids, inhaling the warm, sweet, treacly smell of horse.

'OK, I'm jealous now,' Kian says. 'How come you never bring me apples?'

'I do, sometimes,' I grin. 'It's just that you never tickle my palm while you're eating them.'

'Could be arranged!' Kian makes a dive for my hand, and I swat him away, laughing. Seconds later, he's tickling my face, my neck, my ear, and I'm glad I lied to the dark-haired men this morning, because I need Kian to be here now, with me.

He leans so close to my ear I can feel his breath on my neck, and I know that he's just a heartbeat away from touching me, kissing me. My hair falls across my eyes, but when I shake my head and turn to Kian, he's stopped laughing, his face suddenly distant, distracted. He's looking towards the wishing tree, where the red scarf from this morning flutters out in the breeze.

'My dad,' Kian says slowly. 'My dad's been here.'

Out in the centre of the lough, the little paper boat has sunk without trace.

It's after tea when I hear a muffled yowl of pain from Holly's room. I run through and find her sitting in the middle of the pink quilt with a bag of frozen peas held against her nose. She's shivering and whimpering and chewing her lip.

Then I see the badge, its pin open and bent back at an unnatural angle. One of my old gold studs lies on the quilt, the butterfly clip beside it. I realize that Holly's threats and jokes about piercing her nose were deadly serious.

'What are you *doing*?' I demand, horrified. 'Holly, this is a bad, bad idea!'

'Why?' Holly says through chattering teeth. 'I've got guts, OK? I can do it. It hurts, though – and this is just the ice-pack bit!'

'Holly, can't we talk about this?' I say. 'You're nine. You can't have a pierced nose. And there's no way you can do it yourself! It's crazy!'

'Your friend did it,' Holly points out.

'She was older, and it was ears, not nose,' I argue.

'She was also nuts. I was there, remember? She swore like crazy, and there was a load of blood. Seriously, Holly, bad idea!'

'This will be easier.' Holly grins wickedly. 'Only one piercing to make. You've seen it done – you'll help me, won't you?'

'No way,' I protest. 'Dad and Clare would go crazy.'

Holly lets the packet of frozen peas drop down on to the bed. 'Suppose so,' she says. 'We should be more honest with them, right? We shouldn't have secrets. No piercings, no sneaking out to the lough to meet strange lads . . .'

'Holly!' I say warningly. 'You promised not to tell!'

'Did I?' she says with a shrug. 'Can't remember. No, I think you're right. We shouldn't have secrets from Mum and Chris.'

'Holly, don't do this,' I whisper.

'I want my nose pierced,' she says coolly. 'Are you going to help, or shall I do it myself?'

I have never been blackmailed by a nine-year old before. I pick up the bag of frozen peas and clamp it against Holly's nose, then test the badge pin for sharpness. A bead of bright blood appears at my fingertip. It's sharp, all right.

'Are you sure –' I begin.

'Sure,' Holly snaps. 'Get on with it, before my face gets frostbite.'

I remove the frozen peas and position the badge pin at the side of Holly's nose. It's a cute, tip-tilted, little-girl nose, with just the right amount of freckles scattered across it. I can't imagine it with a stud or a gold ring. It feels wrong.

'Go on!' Holly prompts.

I push the badge pin and she yelps and jumps across the bed, a trickle of red trailing across her top lip. 'Yow!' she shrieks. 'That's sore! Is it done?'

'No – it was just a nick. Come here – and stay still!'

Holly screws her eyes shut and stuffs a corner of the pink quilt into her mouth. I feel bad, like I'm preparing to amputate a leg without anaesthetic.

'Do it!' Holly says from behind the quilt. 'Please, Scarlett!'

So I do. I push the badge pin into her skin, but she jumps again and the badge pin slips and skids down to her top lip, where it slides through the soft skin like a knife through butter.

I have pierced my stepsister's top lip. A thick pool of crimson wells up round the stab wound and snakes down over my shaking hand. I pull the pin out quickly, but by then, Holly is screaming.

'It *hurts*!' she yells. 'Oh, oh, it *hurts*!'

'Shut up!' I hiss, clamping a hand across her mouth. 'Dad and Clare will hear! What did you have to move for? Look what you've made me do! And I told you it would hurt, didn't I? I told you!'

A river of thick, red blood pours down over my hand and drips on to the pink quilt. I sprint out to the bathroom and grab a cold, damp flannel and a box of tissues to staunch the flood.

Holly is crying now, little-girl tears, big gasping shudders of pain and shock. I realize with a sick, shaky certainty that nine is not old enough for this. Nor is nineteen, or even ninety.

'I'm sorry,' I hiss. 'I didn't mean to hurt you. I'm sorry, OK?'

'Is – is it meant to b-bleed this much?' Holly wails, as the blood seeps through the tissue and drips on to her white T-shirt, blooming into a red-rose stain.

'I don't know,' I whisper. 'I can't remember. Shut UP, Holls, for goodness' sake! Please!'

But it's too late.

'Holly?' Clare calls up from the foot of the stairs. 'Scarlett? Is everything OK?'

'Everything's fine,' I shout back. 'No problem.'

But Clare is coming up the stairs. I abandon Holly and step out on to the landing, closing the door behind me.

'Don't worry, Clare,' I tell her, blocking the top of the stairs. 'I yelled, but I'd just banged my toe against the bed in Holly's room. I'm fine now.'

'Oh,' Clare says, 'I was sure it was Holly I heard . . .'

'No, really, Holly's fine,' I argue, but there's a low, shuddering whimper from across the landing and Clare frowns and pushes past me into Holly's room.

It looks like the scene of a small massacre. Holly is curled up on the bed, sobbing raggedly, her arms locked round her face. All around her, spots of blood litter the quilt and scrunched-up, bloodsoaked tissues lie strewn everywhere.

'Dear God,' Clare says. 'What happened?'

'Nothing,' I say. 'It was an accident – tell her, Holly.'

'Oh, Mum,' Holly gasps. 'We used the frozen peas, but it didn't work and the badge pin slipped and it *hurts*! It really, really hurts!'

Clare takes Holly through to the bathroom, tilting her head back as she wipes the blood away and holds a clean white towel against the wound to stop the bleeding. 'Explain,' Clare says to me.

'It wasn't my idea,' I stall. 'I told her it was a bad plan.'

'What was?' Clare demands.

'Piercing her nose.'

'Oh, God,' Clare says. 'It wasn't an accident? She did it herself?'

I look at Clare for a long moment, then I look

at Holly, her green eyes wide and scared, her lips trembling. She looks terrified, but I can't work out whether she's scared of Clare – or me.

My mouth feels dry and my hands are shaking. I've blown it this time, I know. What made me listen to Holly? Messing up your own life, your own body, that's one thing – but wrecking someone else's? That takes real talent.

What made me think this could ever, ever be a good idea? I reach out to hold Holly's hand, but my fingers are sticky, streaked with red. She pulls her hand away.

'Holly didn't do this herself,' I say at last in a quavery voice. 'I did.'

'I'm sorry,' I say, for the seventy-third time in a row. 'It was an accident. I didn't mean to hurt Holly.'

'Didn't mean to hurt her?' Dad flings back, his eyes round with astonishment. 'An accident? Scarlett, spare me the apologies. You've gone too far this time.'

They're just back from an emergency trip to the doctor's surgery in Kilimoor, and Holly is huddled at the table, a clumsy dressing taped to her face. Clare sits next to her, tight-lipped, an arm round Holly's shoulder. Neither of them will look at me.

'I'm sorry,' I repeat.

I've made tea, got the right mugs, even added two sugars to Dad's, but nobody seems to notice. I poured milk for Holly, but she doesn't touch it.

'Sorry doesn't even start to cover it,' Dad snarls. 'Holly is a little girl. She's *nine*, Scarlett. Don't you have any sense of responsibility?'

I wasn't much more than nine when Dad packed

his bags and moved out, but that didn't seem to affect his sense of responsibility. I can think of a million angry retorts to spit back, but I bite my tongue.

'To deliberately puncture her lip – her face – with a dirty old badge pin! What were you thinking of, Scarlett?' Dad rages. 'We've had the wound cleaned, but there could still be infection. And possible scarring. Don't you care about that?'

'Yes, of course I do,' I say as calmly as I can manage.

'And her lip, of all places,' Dad continues. 'What were you trying to do? Make her into – into – a freak? Like you?'

My mouth feels dry and there's a sick, sad feeling in my throat. I can't remember my dad ever saying something so mean, so hurtful.

'Wasn't it bad enough, encouraging her to paint her face and give up meat?' Dad says. 'No. You had to push it one bit further, didn't you? You had to talk her into this!'

'No,' I argue. 'She wanted me to do it. And it was meant to be her nose – the badge pin slipped. I'm sorry!'

'So you say,' Dad retorts. 'I suppose we should be grateful you didn't sever a main artery!'

I glance over at Holly, the injustice of it all bubbling up like the sour taste of guilt. Blackmail, I think. That's why I did it. I wanted to keep Kian a secret, keep my new-found good-girl image, and Holly threatened to blow it all. I can't admit it, though – not now, not ever. Holly could speak out, explain what happened, smooth it all out, but she's acting like I'm some kind of axe murderer, like I meant for this to happen. She stares at the tabletop, slides her hands over her eyes to keep my glare at bay.

It's Clare who looks up and meets my eye. She doesn't look angry, just sad. 'I thought you liked it here,' she says softly. 'I thought you were settling in. I thought you and Holly were friends – that you were good for each other. I thought we could trust you, Scarlett.'

My eyes prick with tears, but I can't cry, I won't. 'You *can* trust me!' I protest. 'It was just a stupid mistake, OK?'

Clare shakes her head. In that one movement, I can see my summer falling apart. I try to see this evening's events through Clare's eyes, and it doesn't look good. It doesn't look good at all.

'You *can* trust me,' I say in a small voice. 'I'm happy here.' But Clare turns her face away, and I can feel that happiness slipping away, falling through my fingers like sand.

I chuck some stuff into the fluffy backpack, layer on a fleece and a jacket, slip on my ugly, sensible sandals. I pocket a handful of euros from my dressing table, a chocolate bar left over from earlier. I creep down the stairs, avoiding the squeaky step three from the bottom, but still a door creaks open on the landing. When I look up, Holly is looking down over the banisters, her hair sticking out like straw, her eyes heavy with sleep. The dressing has come away from her wound in the night, and I can see the beginnings of a dark red scab just centimetres from her mouth.

'Terrible place for a stud,' I say, and Holly smiles faintly, just a flicker of something that might be forgiveness.

'Don't go,' she whispers.

I put a finger to my lips, then turn away.

The lane is spooky at night. An owl hoots in the distance, and there's a noise beyond the hedge that sounds like an old man coughing, although I think it's only sheep.

I've messed up plenty of times in my life, but this time I've done it with style.

What did it matter, anyhow, messing up at school? There was always going to be another place, another bunch of teachers to annoy, another gang of bad-girl friends. What did it matter, dyeing my hair red, piercing my tongue, clomping through the streets on three-inch wedges? Nobody was looking, anyway. Nobody cared.

Mum would just huff and stress and pack me off somewhere safely out of sight, then change her mind and decide it was all a fuss about nothing. Back I'd come to carry on like nothing ever happened. Not this time, though. This time, it's different.

I thought it'd be the worst thing in the world,

being sent to this middle-of-nowhere hole to live with Dad and Clare and Holly. I wanted to hate them, and I tried, I really did, but I just couldn't. I walked into that cheesy little cottage and even though I was angrier than I've ever been, I could feel the happiness there. I guess I just wanted to be a part of it. Some chance of that now.

I slip through the gap in the hedge and into the woods, my feet crunching through broken twigs and last year's dried leaves. All those years, I thought that my Dad was a total loser. Now I know he was just a guy in an unhappy marriage, a guy who fell for someone else and took his chance of happiness. Can I blame him for that? Not really. After all, when I thought I could have that happiness, too, all the anger dropped away and I grabbed for it with both hands. I nearly had it, too.

The trouble is, I've had no practice at being a big sister. I wanted to make Holly happy. I wanted her to think I was cool and wild and clever, and I let myself be blackmailed. Would she really have told Dad and Clare about Kian? I don't think so. Not Holly.

Don't go, she said, but it's not like I have a choice. I can't stay there now, because they know how stupid, how bad, I really am. Bad enough to stab my little stepsister through the lip.

It's not like that's all, either. I need to find Kian.

I was wrong to stay silent about the dark-haired men who were looking for him, and I need to put that right before I go.

He's down by the lough, a hunched figure in the darkness. He is sitting on a rock beside the water, next to a small fire edged with stones and fuelled with fallen branches. An empty tin of beans, blackened on the outside, lies in the embers, and Midnight stands at a distance, gazing out across the lough.

'Hey,' he says, as though it's the most natural thing in the world for me to come strolling out of the woods at past one in the morning.

'Hey, yourself.' I sit down beside him, hugging my knees, holding my hands out to the fire. 'Don't you ever sleep?'

'Sometimes.' He laughs. 'I've just been sitting, thinking, that's all. I kind of lost track of time.'

My eyes slide over to the wishing tree, to the long scarf the dark-haired man in the hat tied on to a branch this morning. I can see it silhouetted against the night sky.

'Some guys came to the lough this morning, looking for you,' I say in a rush. 'Two dark-haired guys, one with a hat, one with a moustache. I didn't know what to say, so I pretended I didn't know you, and they went away. The younger one tied a scarf on to the wishing tree.'

'Yeah.' Kian sighs. 'My dad. My dad and my uncle.'

'I should have told you,' I say. 'I'm sorry. I was going to, but then you saw the scarf and I thought it didn't matter any more.'

Kian sighs. 'It doesn't matter, Scarlett,' he says. 'At least I know they were here, they were looking.'

'Looks like we're both in trouble,' I say heavily. 'I can't stay here any more. I messed up at Dad's, hurt Holly.'

'You hurt her?' Kian repeats.

'It was an accident, but yeah, it was my fault,' I say. 'They know what I'm like now. I'm trouble, I'm hopeless. It's time to move on.'

Kian stares into the fire, his face highlighted in the dull red glow. I guess this is the bit where I want him to suggest we run away together, away from the dark-haired men, away from Dad and Clare and Holly. We could ride Midnight up into the hills, find a ruined cottage and live there in secret – just us, no school, no adults, no hassle.

'Scarlett, you're not going anywhere,' Kian says. 'You just made a mistake. They'll forgive you – they'll get over it.'

'They won't,' I say in a small voice. 'I've let them down.'

'You would if you ran away,' Kian says.

The injustice of this hits me like a slap. 'It's OK

for you, though, isn't it?' I fling at him. 'To run away? To let people down? Your dad and your uncle, they were looking for you. This wasn't the first place they looked and it won't be the last, either. They were sad – your dad especially. They wanted to find you. So don't preach at me about running away! You did it yourself!'

Kian looks at me, his face shadowed. 'I did, I know, but you don't know the reason for it,' he says. 'It's a good reason, OK? Not just some family squabble that could be patched up if you'd just grow up and sit tight and accept that you were wrong.'

'It's not like that!' I splutter.

'Isn't it?'

I'm so angry I'd like to slap his face, thump my fists against his skinny chest, spit on his shoes. Instead, I take a big breath in and count to ten, but that doesn't even start to cut it, and I'm at eighty-seven before I feel his hand snake round mine in the dark.

'I thought you'd understand,' I whisper.

'I do understand,' he says. 'I know that running away is a bad idea. It's the worst, OK? Look, Scarlett, something happened – something I just can't talk about. It's been eating me up, and I ran away, came here, trying to get my head straight. I know how much I've hurt my family, worried them. And I know I have to go back.'

'Go back?' I panic. 'You can't!'

'Scarlett, I wouldn't have stayed this long if it hadn't been for you,' Kian says.

We sit in the dark for a long time in silence, holding hands, until the fire dies down to softly glowing embers.

'We have to do this, even though it's tough,' Kian says. 'I have to go back, and you have to stay here, face up to what you did, make your family see that you're sorry.'

'I can't.'

'You can, Scarlett,' Kian tells me. 'You're strong. You've made mistakes, sure, but running away would be the biggest one of all, I promise.'

Later, we ride back through the woods and along the lane, Kian's arms round me, our hands muddled up together in Midnight's mane.

'I don't want you to go,' I whisper. 'Please don't.'

'I have to,' Kian sighs.

'Just a few more days? Please?' I beg. 'You haven't finished the hayricks, yet, you said . . .'

'I dunno,' he says. 'I really need to find my dad and uncle. It's important.'

'I know, of course,' I tell him. 'But just a day or two? To say goodbye?'

Kian is silent for a long time, and then he speaks softly, quietly, into my hair. 'Just a day or two then. OK?'

'Promise?'

'Promise.'

We've reached the cottage gate with Holly's handpainted sign advertizing eggs and strawberries and lettuce. I slip down from Midnight's back and turn towards the house. The curtain in Holly's room twitches slightly.

'I'll do the hayricks first thing,' he tells me. 'Meet you at the lough at one o'clock? At least we can say goodbye.'

I nod in the darkness, glad he can't see my stricken face, then turn away quickly as he turns Midnight round, back towards the lough. I sneak round the side of the cottage, slip in through the back door, creep up the stairs. As I cross the landing, I hear Holly's door shut softly, see the light click off from inside.

I knock softly on her door, turn the handle, go inside. She's pretending to sleep, her face pale against the gloom, the quilt drawn up to her chin. I bend down to touch her cheek and she sits up, throwing her arms round me, hugging me so tightly I can hardly breathe.

'Oh, Scarlett,' she says. 'I thought you'd gone.'

In the morning, Dad takes Holly into Galway to the dentist. There's some dispute over whether she's well enough, but I get the feeling Dad wants to keep her out of my way. The heat is already stifling outside, but things are feeling distinctly frosty between Dad, Clare and me.

'Sorry,' I say again.

'S'OK.' Holly grins. 'I've changed my mind, anyhow. I don't want a piercing any more.'

'Bit late for that,' Dad huffs. 'Thanks to Scarlett.'

I am sorry, though. Sorry enough to take Kian's advice and come back, sorry enough to hang around and watch the icicles form around me as Dad flashes me a reproachful look and Clare eyes me warily, as though I might start hacking the kitchen to bits with the bread knife at any moment.

Dad and Holly head off in the Morris Traveller. They're making soap deliveries to craft shops in Galway too, and Dad has a meeting with a business that makes rag dolls from organic wool and cotton, and wants a handknitted website to match. They'll be away all day.

'I'll be in the workshop if you need me,' Clare says curtly. There's no warmth, no sympathy in her voice, just a quiver of hurt, confusion. I know I put that there, and it makes me feel bad.

There's more than one way to say sorry, though. I get out the mixing bowl and make a batch of fairy cakes, icing the tops with buttercream and decorating them with ripe strawberries from the garden. I do the washing up, mop the kitchen floor, then work for a while on my project folder. It's so hot now, even inside the cottage, that a trickle of sweat slips down the small of my back.

What will Kian be doing now? Making hayricks in the scorching heat. It's not even half ten. I don't think I can survive till one o'clock.

I open the fridge and see a jug of Clare's home-made lemonade tucked away at the back. I pour myself a glass, and, as an afterthought, one for Clare. I add a couple of cubes of ice and take it out to the workshop.

The smell of crushed strawberries and fresh mint hits me as I open the door, and Clare looks up from a bowl of freshly liquidized fruit. This is her territory, and I've been careful to avoid it before today; my eyes flick around the room, taking in shelves stacked with pans, jars of mysterious powders, oils and granules. In the corner, a big pan filled with molten soap is cooling.

'Lemonade?' I say shyly, setting the drink down on the table. 'It's so hot, I thought you'd need something.'

'Thanks, ' Clare says, taking a long drink. 'That was thoughtful.'

'Is there anything I can do to help?'

Clare looks startled, then faintly horrified. I have never offered to help her with the soap before. She frowns, then shrugs and chucks me an apron. 'Why not?' she says. 'You can grease the moulds for me – it's like greasing a cake tin.'

I set to work while Clare gives the fruit and mint a final whizz. She finishes off her lemonade, puts on rubber gloves and goggles and weighs out a heap of white granules.

'This is caustic soda, pretty strong stuff,' Clare says. 'Open that window as wide as it'll go, would you? And stay over there.'

'Why, what happens?'

Clare ties a scarf over her nose and mouth so that she looks like a pregnant bank robber, then tips the granules into the fruity liquid. A cloud of fumes rise up from the mixture, prickling my nose.

'You can't put stuff like that in soap,' I protest. 'It'd burn the face off you!'

Clare shakes her head and the scarf slips down

round her neck. 'Ah, but when we blend this into the vegetable fat mixture, there's a chemical reaction. The soda gets neutralized – it disappears, if you like.'

'I didn't realize it was so complicated,' I say, impressed.

'Ah, it's a real mad professor's laboratory in here,' Clare says.

She pours the strawberry and mint into the cauldron of soap, and starts stirring. 'It'll take a while to reach trace point,' she tells me. 'Meanwhile we can take this little lot out of its moulds . . .'

She chucks me a pair of rubber gloves and I set to work turning out slabs of what looks and smells like coconut ice – the soap has been layered with white on the bottom and pink on top. Clare trims each slab and cuts it neatly into squares with a cheese slice, for me to stack and cover with a blanket to 'cure'.

'I don't like this weather,' Clare frowns. 'It's really close and sticky, even with the window open. I feel like I've done a whole day's work already. I think there'll be thunder, later.'

I give the strawberry mixture a stir. 'Hope not,' I say. 'I wanted to go down to the lough.'

'You love that lough, don't you?' Clare says. 'I have to admit, you've worked really hard on that project of yours, even in the school holidays. That's something to be proud of.'

166

Would she still think that if she knew the real reason I love being by the lough? So I can hang out with a runaway boy, a bad boy, a boy I'm going to miss like crazy. Nope, she'd think I was bad beyond hope.

'Clare, I'm sorry about what happened with Holly,' I say into the silence. 'Really sorry. OK?'

'I know that, Scarlett,' she says softly. 'OK. That's trace point for the soap – time to add the colouring and fragrance.'

I stir in diluted red colouring and watch the soap change from speckled pink to deep, vivid red. Next, I measure out strawberry and peppermint oil, mix it up and stand back as Clare ladles the liquid soap into the moulds. A film of sweat glistens on her brow and she catches her lip as she dips and pours the mixture. She is almost eight months' pregnant, and she shouldn't be doing this, not in this heat.

'Let's call it a day,' I suggest when the last mould has been filled and the cauldron, ladle and measuring jug have been set to soak in the sink. 'It's way too hot to work.'

'Perhaps you're right,' Clare says uncertainly.

Outside the window, the first crash of thunder booms out across the valley.

The rain starts then, slowly at first, big drops of rain that spatter my hand as I reach out to pull the window closed. By the time Clare has tidied the workbench, it's pelting down, hammering against the workshop's tin roof.

'This has been threatening all week,' Clare says, draping blankets over the freshly poured trays of soap. 'At least the storm will clear the air.'

I frown. 'I hope Dad and Holly are OK in Galway.'

'Might not even be raining there,' Clare says. 'The valley has much more dramatic weather than the rest of the area, because of the lough and the mountains. We get these storms sometimes. It's not really surprising after all that hot weather – should have known it wouldn't last!'

We pull the door shut behind us and run across the grass to the house. The rain lashes us with icy fingers, pelting our hair, running down our bare arms in tiny rivulets. By the time we get inside, we're drenched. Clare chucks me a towel and I rub at my hair, heading upstairs to change. I pick out a black top and a short, red, wraparound skirt. When I come back down, Clare has the patchwork cot quilt spread out over her knees and a bag of scrap fabric spilt out across the table. Two more lemonades sit side by side next to the scrap-bag.

'Thanks, Clare.'

I pick up my drink and drift over to the window. The rain is sluicing down so fast I can barely see out – my plans to spend the afternoon by the lough with Kian are not looking good. A new crash of thunder makes me step back from the window.

'It's getting closer,' I say. 'I hope the chickens will be OK.'

'They've coped with worse than this,' Clare tells me. 'They won't like it, of course, but these storms never last too long. Don't worry, Scarlett.'

It's silly, I know, but I was really scared of thunderstorms when I was a kid. Now I know that there's nothing really to be scared of, but still, each flash of lightning and crash of thunder twists my insides a little. I sit down at the table, sipping my drink, and open my maths book at a fresh chapter.

I've been staring at the first problem for a whole five minutes when Clare takes the book away and closes it gently.

'Help me, instead,' she says. 'It'll take your mind off things.'

'I'm fine,' I protest.

'I know you are,' Clare says lightly. 'It's just that I could do with some advice. I've almost finished this, but it still looks a bit flat and ordinary. It needs something else – I just don't know what!'

I spread the quilt out across the table. It's beautiful – a tiny patchwork of random shapes and colours, overstitched with bright embroidery threads. I can see the pale blue stripes of Holly's outgrown school dress, a washed-out scrap of denim from an old pair of Dad's jeans, a pastel floral print that has to be cut from something of Clare's. Bits and pieces of their lives are stitched into this quilt, pieced together to make the new baby warm and welcome.

'It needs more colour,' Clare says decisively. 'Something strong and vivid to frame the paler scraps. A border – red maybe?'

The thunder booms again outside, rattling the windowpanes.

'I – I'd like to put something into the quilt,' I say softly. 'I know I'm not a proper sister, but . . .'

'Scarlett, you are!' Clare exclaims. 'You're going to be this baby's half-sister, exactly like Holly. I'd *love* you to contribute something to the quilt. I've wanted to ask you a hundred times, but I was scared you'd say no . . .'

'I would have said no,' I admit. 'I didn't want to be part of this family, or part of this project, not to start with. But – well, I feel differently now. It's not too late, is it?'

Clare puts a hand out to touch my cheek. 'It's not too late at all,' she says. 'How could it be? Thank you, Scarlett.'

'You could have a bit of this,' I say, pulling at my red skirt. 'Or maybe my burgundy combats? What d'you think?'

'Ah, no,' Clare says. 'You can't cut them up, it'd be such a waste!'

I shrug. 'I don't have any old clothes with me, though.'

'Unless . . . Well, there's the stuff in the attic,' Clare says.

The thunder crashes again, and the kitchen light flickers slightly and then steadies. 'What stuff in the attic?' I ask. 'There's nothing of mine up there.'

Clare hesitates, biting her lip. She can't quite meet my eye.

'Clare?'

'Actually, there is,' she says at last. 'Sacks and sacks of stuff that your Dad's kept hold of for years, since you moved out of the house in Islington. I think he was supposed to be taking it to the charity shop, but he made the mistake of looking in the bin bags, and he just couldn't bear to part with it.'

My head is spinning. What was in those bin bags, all that time ago? Toys, clothes, books – bits and pieces of my childhood. When Dad left, I threw out everything I could from the old days. Getting rid of the memories wasn't so easy . . .

'He kept it all?' I ask. 'Everything?'

'I think so,' Clare tells me. 'I'm sorry, Scarlett. He should have told you.'

The lights flicker off and on again, and I rub my forehead, trying to clear the fog from my mind. My childhood, neatly bagged up, is sitting in the attic above our heads. It's not lost, after all.

'Can I see it?' I ask. 'The stuff in the attic?'

Clare grins. 'Of course, Scarlett. Fetch that stepladder from the back porch, would you? I'll show you exactly where it is . . .'

We go up the stairs, carrying the wooden stepladder between us. On the landing, Clare opens up the rickety stepladder below the square wooden hatch in the ceiling and climbs up, pushing the hatch door open to reveal a dark, cavernous space.

'Lucky there's a light up here,' she calls, flicking the switch on.

'Come down,' I call. 'It doesn't look safe. You hold the ladder and I'll go up.'

'Nonsense!' Clare laughs, tanned feet in flowery

flip-flops disappearing up the rungs of the ladder. 'I'm pregnant, not ill. Come on!'

I follow her up into the floored loft space, piled high with boxes, tea chests, rolls of carpet and black bin bags. My heart starts to thump.

Clare is already kneeling beside the black bin bags, opening the knots at the top and checking inside them. 'That's them,' she says. 'One, two, three . . . four. Do you want to see? It's your stuff really, so if there's anything you want we can throw it down.'

I look inside the first bin bag, fishing out school books, plimsolls, a stack of dog-eared pony books. There's a bundle of home-made cards tied up with string, carefully coloured with stubby wax crayons or scratchy pencils or garish felt pens, endless sketches of ponies, a green potato-shaped car that has to be the Morris Traveller.

Inside the second I find a bag of Barbie dolls, a black Barbie horse with red wool plaited into the mane, my very first pair of satin ballet shoes and an impossibly tiny pink leotard. The third bin bag is stuffed with soft toys – a fleecy brown bear, a ragged panda with only one ear, a knitted donkey that Gran made me back in the days when I was still her favourite granddaughter and not the problem child from hell.

How did it all go so wrong?

I'm taking big breaths in, yet the air seems thick and soupy and I can't quite fill my lungs. I'm trying hard to stop my hands from shaking, and my eyes sting, either with dust or tears, I can't tell.

'Scarlett?' Clare puts an arm round me, and I wipe a hand against my eyes. The fourth bag holds clothes. On top there's the red velvet dress I wore on my eighth birthday, then the cerise silk crinkle-skirt I wore on holiday in Corfu. There's a red fluffy jumper, the one I wore when we went to see *The Nutcracker*, the Christmas I was six, and the crimson corduroy pinafore dress I loved so much when I was five. We pull out dress after dress, a dozen different kinds of red, shades of scarlet, ruby, burgundy, crimson, each one soft velvet or thick wool, embroidered cotton or crumpled linen.

'Red was my favourite colour,' I whisper.

Clare strokes my hair. 'I think that's what I was remembering,' she tells me. 'All the little red dresses. But you need to keep these, Scarlett – I wouldn't dream of asking you to cut them up. They're special, aren't they?'

My throat is aching, and I can't quite find the words to explain just how special these bin bags full of memories really are. I just nod and smile and hug the dresses, breathing in a long-forgotten smell of lemony washing powder and happiness.

'They're special,' I say to Clare when I can speak

again. 'That's why I want to use some of them for the quilt, OK? Please, Clare? It's the best thing I can give to the new baby. My baby brother or sister.'

Clare hugs me, and I don't pull away. It's only when the thunder crashes again, right above our heads, that we break apart. 'Goodness, if this storm gets any closer it'll be right inside the attic!' Clare exclaims. 'Let's get back downstairs.'

I pick out two or three of the little red dresses and throw them down through the open hatch, watching them flutter down on to the landing carpet.

I climb down first, hands holding tight to the smooth, paint-spattered wood of the ladder. Once my feet are firmly on the floor again, I hold the ladder steady for Clare. Looking up, I see her legs lowering shakily down, her brown feet in flip-flops feeling about for the rungs.

Then there's a loud bang from downstairs and the lights go out, leaving us in semi-darkness. A roar of thunder rumbles out above our heads, and suddenly there's a scream and Clare is falling. I put my hands out to catch her, but my hands close round the crinkly fabric of her skirt, which tears from my grasp. She falls heavily against the ladder, then twists to the side and lands with a sickening thud on the carpet, red velvet and crimson silk all around her.

'Clare?' I whimper, my voice so small and scared I barely recognize it. 'Clare? Are you all right?'

Clare is still and silent. She's lying awkwardly, her head at an angle against the skirting board, blonde curls spread out around her. She looks very pale.

'Clare,' I hiss urgently. 'Please wake up. Talk to me, Clare!'

Panic rises up inside me, a tidal wave of fear. I don't know what to do. A voice in my head tells me you're not supposed to move people who've hurt themselves, but it can't be right to leave her squashed in against the wall like that. I tug her shoulders, pulling her away from the wall so her head can rest more easily. As I straighten the hair at her temple, my hand touches something warm and wet. Blood.

I feel like I'm falling down a deep, dark well, and I know there'll be snakes and sharks at the bottom. Then, abruptly, Clare speaks.

'Ow,' she says, her eyes fluttering open. 'What the heck happened there?'

'Clare!' I gasp, my body slumping with relief. 'You're OK!'

I put my arms round her and help her to sit up. She leans back against the wall, a hand pressed against her temple. 'I don't feel like I'm OK,' she says in a shaky voice. 'I feel like I just got run over by a truck.' She squints around her in the dim light. 'I'm on the landing?' she asks, puzzled. 'What did I do?'

'The lights went out – it's a power cut,' I explain. 'Something to do with the storm. You were coming down the ladder from the attic, and you lost your footing. Remember?'

Clare frowns. 'Not really . . . I fell off a ladder?'

'We were in the attic, sorting through clothes for the patchwork cot quilt,' I tell her. 'My fault, really. Stupid thing to do in a storm.'

As we listen, there's a distant rumble of thunder, less angry now. The storm is passing.

I pick up one of Clare's flip-flops from across the landing. 'These probably didn't help,' I tell her. 'It's OK, Clare. You'll feel better in a minute. It was just a shock.' I have no idea if this is true, but it sounds reassuring. Right now, both of us could do with that.

'Every bit of me hurts,' Clare murmurs. She

curves her arms around her bulging tummy and a new fear hits me. My mouth feels dry.

'Clare, is the baby OK?' I ask. 'Can you tell? The baby's OK, right?'

Clare takes my hand and rests it on her belly, and I feel a sudden movement, like ripples underwater, beneath the floral print of her dress. 'He's kicking,' she whispers. 'Or she. The baby's fine, just mad at me for giving him such a jolt.'

'Thank goodness for that. You scared me, Clare,' I tell her. 'I thought you were really hurt!'

She looks at me, a smile twitching her lips. 'I think I'll be black and blue in the morning, and I do feel kind of hazy about what happened, but I guess I'll live.'

'Are you OK to stand up?' I ask, and with an effort and some help from me, Clare gets to her feet slowly.

'No bones broken,' she says a little shakily.

'It was a nasty fall,' I say. 'You gave me a fright. You'll be fine now, though. And Dad'll know what to do, when he gets back.'

Clare leans heavily on the landing banister, looking kind of vague. 'That's right. Chris will be back soon,' she says. 'Where did you say he's gone?'

'He's in Galway,' I tell her. 'With Holly, remember? They'll be back by teatime. Dad can run you to the doctor's, get you checked out.'

'Ah, sure,' Clare says. 'I'll be fine, just fine. They'll be back any minute.'

But it's barely lunchtime, and Dad and Holly won't be back for hours. I make a decision to ring him on the mobile he keeps in the car for emergencies. This is one, loud and clear, and I'm way out of my depth.

We take the stairs one at a time, side by side, arms round each other for support. Halfway down, Clare stops, her face creased with pain. Her breathing seems shallow, and her eyes flutter closed.

'Clare?' I panic. 'Clare, what's wrong?'

'Ah, it's nothing,' she says, her face relaxed again. 'Just a little twinge, so.'

We go on, step by step, until we reach the bottom, and I lead Clare across to the kitchen table, still littered with scraps of fabric and threads. She falls into a chair, and I grab a clean tea towel and dip it in warm water to clean up her cut. When I turn, though, she's doubled up in pain, her face grey.

'What is it?' I demand. 'Clare, what's hurting? Shall I ring a doctor?'

Clare straightens up, taking a deep breath in. 'I think you should.' She frowns. 'Call Chris, or the doctor. I'm not sure I'm feeling too great.'

I try not to panic, but my fingers tremble as I grab the phone off the wall and punch out Dad's mobile number from the list of useful numbers taped to the wall. I hold the receiver to my ear, but there's no dialling tone, nothing at all. I must have dialled it wrong, or perhaps Dad has his mobile switched off.

I try the doctor's number, more carefully this time, but again the line is dead. I put the receiver down and pick it up again, rattle the cradle, shake the receiver. The whole phone is dead, totally.

'Clare, it's not working,' I say as calmly as I can. 'The line is dead. The storm must have knocked the phone out too. What shall I do?'

Clare is hunched over again, her whole body rigid with a new wave of pain. I reach out, grab her hand and squeeze it tight, and she squeezes back, so hard it hurts.

Then the moment has passed and she looks up, her face relaxed again, eyes soft and heavy. 'I think I'd like to lie down,' she says. 'I'm so tired. I'll just close my eyes, and everything will be better . . .'

A memory surfaces, something from a long-ago school playtime when a boy called Roddy Mitchell fell over and banged his head, hard. The teachers called an ambulance and sat talking to him, keeping him awake, refusing to let him drift off into sleep. 'He's concussed,' our teacher had explained. 'Sleep is the very last thing he needs right now.'

'No, sleeping's not a good idea,' I say to Clare.

'Not after that fall. You lost consciousness for a bit back there, and you could be concussed or something. I'm sure you're supposed to stay awake, keep talking, until we can get you to a doctor.'

'Oh yes, a doctor,' Clare says, her voice dreamy, distant. 'You'd better get a doctor. I think I'm in labour, Scarlett – the baby's coming.'

The electricity's gone, the phone line is dead and Clare is bruised, concussed and in labour at not quite eight months' pregnant. The baby isn't due until the end of August. This is bad – seriously bad.

We are in the middle of nowhere. There are no neighbours, nobody to help. We're eight miles from the nearest village, more than thirty from the hospital, and Dad and Holly are miles away in Galway, delivering boxes of lemon-zinger soap and eating pizza for lunch.

'Clare, what shall I do?' I whine again, but Clare is lost in her own world, drifting somewhere between pain and sleep.

'Open your eyes!' I tell her. 'Get up, Clare! It's important! You need to stay awake, keep walking, OK?'

'OK,' she says hazily.

We walk round the kitchen a few times until Clare is halted by another contraction. She gives a low, animal groan that makes me shudder, and I realize that unless I do something fast I'm going to be delivering this baby myself, on the kitchen floor.

'I'll get help,' I promise Clare. 'I'll find somebody, get us to the hospital, OK? I won't be long. Keep walking, OK? Stay awake.'

It's just past one, and Kian will be at the lough, waiting for me. He'll know what to do. Clare looks at me in horror as I open the door, step out into the rain. 'Please stay!' she whimpers.

I feel torn, but I have no choice – I need to get help.

I run down the lane, splashing through puddles, brushing against the wet leaves of the fuchsia hedge. It's still raining, and by the time I reach the edge of the woods my clothes are soaked. I plunge into the trees, stumbling over the roots and stumps, hurtling down to the lough. A branch catches the hem of my red skirt, ripping it slightly, but I don't stop running.

'*Kian!*' I scream as I run. 'Kian, help!'

Any minute, he'll hear me, he'll come riding through the trees on Midnight, and they can go for help while I wait with Clare. Any minute.

'Kian!' I shout, my lungs burning. 'Kian, where are you? Help me, please!'

I stumble out of the woods on to the grass at

the water's edge. Kian is not there. I scan the hillside, rain running down my face. There is no sign of Kian, or Midnight. The lough is deserted, silent and brooding under the darkened sky. No fishermen, no tourists, nobody at all.

I stand still, my breath coming in gasps. He said he'd be here – he promised. Kian has always been here when I needed him. Today, though, when it really, really matters, I'm on my own. Maybe he's hauling canvas over new-made hayricks, or sheltering with Midnight until the storm passes. He'll be here soon. So why does the lough feel so silent, so deserted?

My eyes fix on to the wishing tree, searching through the rags and ribbons that hang heavy, dripping, from its branches. My heart is pounding. I tear at the branches, pulling them out of the way, until I can see the forked branches in the centre of the tree where Kian's rucksack should sit. There's no rucksack, no bedroll, nothing, just a wisp of wet hay clinging on to a branch.

Everything's gone.

I wasn't worth a promise, an extra day, not even a goodbye. I want to scream, I want to howl, I want to lie down on the wet grass and never get up, but there's no time for any of that. I have to be strong because Clare needs me. I have to help her, because there's nobody else to do it.

I tear a strip of ripped red fabric from the hem of my skirt and tie it on to the highest branch I can reach. 'Please,' I'm whispering into the hazel leaves. 'Please let Clare be OK. Let the baby survive. Let it all work out, please, please . . .'

But the tree just shakes rain down on me, and I turn away, helpless. I run back through the woods and out on to the lane, and by the time I reach the gate the clouds are lifting and a few bright rays of sun shine through.

Beyond the dripping fuchsia hedges to my left, in the distance, a shimmering rainbow arches across the valley, and as I stare at last my heart lifts. I can hear something, in the distance . . . the hum of a car motor.

All I can do is step out into the middle of the lane, drenched, my breath coming in gasps. The engine sound gets louder, and after an eternity a red Skoda swerves into sight. 'Stop!' I shout, running drunkenly towards the bonnet. 'Please, please stop!'

The car slows, coming to a halt right beside the gate. I stagger over to the driver's door, wait for the window to buzz down.

'Hi there,' says an American tourist in a palm-tree print shirt, grinning widely. 'Some weather you get around these parts, huh?'

Beside him, a middle-aged blonde in a pink

T-shirt leans over, pointing to the sign on the gate. Holly's cardboard notice, drawn out in a dozen different felt-pen colours, is all smeared and running in the rain.

'Honey,' the blonde woman says. 'We've come to buy eggs. We bought some last week from the little girl with the bunches. Best eggs we've ever eaten. We'll take another dozen, please.'

Her husband frowns, looking me up and down. 'Say,' he says slowly. 'Are you OK?'

The American tourists are called Ed and Sylvie, and they are driving Clare and me to Castlebar Hospital. Sylvie sits in the back with Clare, mopping her face with wet wipes and telling her to breathe, while I struggle with the road map in the passenger seat, directing Ed through the lanes, past Kilimoor and on towards Castlebar.

'Stay calm, kid,' he tells me, snapping his gum. 'Sylvie has had four littl'uns of her own. She knows all about this childbirth business.'

'Most natural thing in the world,' Sylvie says. 'My third, now he came early too, and kinda unexpected. Three pounds eleven ounces, he was – he's six foot two now, and running his own company! Just keep breathing, Clare. Don't worry 'bout a thing.'

'I'll be fine,' Clare says shakily from the back. 'Really, Scarlett. I'm sorry to frighten you.'

'You didn't!' I protest. 'I was worried, that's all. You kept going all woozy and sleepy on me, and then when the baby started I just didn't know what to do . . .'

'You did fine,' Clare reassures me, and then takes a deep breath in as a fresh wave of pain hits her.

'Breathe, honey,' Sylvie tells her. 'Breathe through the pain. There . . . Now relax. The contractions are still around five minutes apart, so there's no need to panic just yet. We'll get you to the hospital, honey – everything's gonna be just fine.'

Clare's hand reaches forward to stroke my hair. 'Stop worrying, Scarlett,' she says. 'I felt really woozy back there, but my head's much clearer now. I've got a splitting headache, though. Maybe it'll take my mind off the contractions!'

'They won't know which bit of you to check out first,' Sylvie laughs, 'but you seem OK to me. Didn't anyone tell you not to go climbing ladders when you're thirty-four weeks pregnant?'

'My fault,' I say gloomily. 'I should have stopped you.'

'Nobody's fault,' Clare corrects me. 'I'd have been fine if it hadn't been for the power cut.'

'And the flip-flops,' I remind her.

'And the flip-flops. OK, so maybe that bit was my fault,' Clare admits. 'Never, never blame yourself, though, Scarlett. Promise me that . . .' Her voice trails off as another wave of pain hits.

'Try that phone again,' Ed tells me.

I go back to punching numbers into Ed's mobile. Dad's number is still dead – his mobile must be switched off – but after a few attempts I get through to the hospital and begin a garbled explanation of what's happening.

'Tell them the contractions are five minutes apart,' Sylvie instructs, and I pass on the information. The duty nurse wants to know how far we are from Castlebar.

'Ten, fifteen miles?' I hazard, frowning at the map. She tells us to drive safely, and that they'll be ready for us as soon as we arrive, a midwife and doctor standing by. I end the call.

There's some murmuring in the back of the car. When Clare looks up, surfacing from yet another contraction, she looks lost and anxious, her face pale, lips grey.

'Ed, honey,' Sylvie says, 'I don't really want to deliver this baby in a hire car by the side of the road. Be an angel and step on the gas, would you?'

29

The maternity wing smells of disinfectant and hope. I sit on a blue vinyl chair in the waiting area, Ed at my side, his big palm-patterned presence calming, comforting. Sylvie has gone off to fetch coffee, which she says will make everyone feel better. Clare is in the delivery suite with the doctor and the midwife. Groans of pain drift out now and again, to reassure us all that the labour is progressing.

I flip open Ed's mobile and punch Dad's number in yet again. Why have a mobile if you never switch it on? It's infuriating. What if I can't get through at all, and Dad and Holly arrive back at the cottage to find the place deserted, not even a scribbled note on the kitchen table?

I hold the mobile to my ear and as if by magic, this time the call rings through.

'Hello, Chris Flynn's mobile, how may I help you?' a chirpy voice says.

'Holly, let me speak to Dad,' I bark.

'Oh, hi, Scarlett,' she says. 'I'm in the dentist's waiting room, playing Snake on the mobile –'

'It's an emergency, Holly,' I tell her. 'Let me speak to Dad, OK?'

'Scarlett?' Dad's voice comes on to the line. 'What is it?'

'Dad, I've been trying to get you for ages,' I blurt. 'You have to come, quickly. Clare fell off a ladder and hurt her head, and there was a terrible storm and two Americans gave us a lift to Castlebar Hospital. The doctors think everything is fine but you'd better come quickly, Dad, because she's having the baby, OK?'

There's a silence at the other end. 'She's having the *baby*?' Dad says carefully.

'Yes, I said so, didn't I?'

There's a muffled crash at the other end of the line, and then Holly's voice is back. 'He dropped it into a potted plant,' she says, exasperated. 'Lucky I'm here to take charge of things. It's almost time for my appointment, but I guess those fillings will have to wait. Shame. We're on our way, Scarlett, OK? Tell Mum to hold on. We'll be there as soon as we can.'

The doctor comes out to talk to us. He says Clare is in good shape, and that the monitors show the baby's heartbeat is strong.

'We've got a message through to the father,' Ed chips in. 'He'll be here just as soon as it's humanly possible. An hour maybe?'

'A lot can happen in an hour,' the doctor says. 'Clare's asking for you, Scarlett, and you, Sylvie. If the father doesn't get here in time, how d'you feel about being Clare's birth partners?'

Sylvie beams. 'Try and stop us.'

I say nothing. I can think of about a million reasons why I shouldn't walk through that door. I'm clueless about childbirth and babies. When we had that sex education film at school, I pretended I was sick at the childbirth bit and hid out in the girls' loos writing rude things about Mrs Mulhern on the cubicle door.

I don't like pain and I can't stand the sight of blood, I hate hospitals and it's not even like Clare is any relation to me, not really. I'd be better staying out of it, seriously.

'Scarlett?' the doctor says. 'She really wants you with her.'

I take a deep breath and all in a rush I remember that it's Clare in there, and that she needs me. I can't let her down. In the delivery room, Clare is kneeling on the bed, hanging on to the metal rails at its foot. She is wearing a weird hospital nightie and the look of someone who is battling hard.

Sylvie strokes her forehead with the wet wipes,

and I hold her hand, telling her to hang on, Dad's coming, and Holly. The midwife bustles around us, checking the monitor, resting her hand on Clare's stomach with each contraction. Outside the sun is shining, like there never was a storm or an accident at all.

The contractions are so long and strong now that each one seems to merge into the next. Clare has been given a tube to gulp down gas and air as each new wave of pain hits, but still she grabs on to me, her hands clawing into mine as she struggles back from each onslaught.

'I'm sorry, Scarlett,' she grins, her face red with effort and damp with sweat. 'I didn't plan on this.'

'It's OK,' I tell her. 'You're doing great, Clare. Keep going! Count to ten and remember to breathe!'

Clare laughs, even through the pain. 'Now where have I heard that before?'

'C'mon, honey,' Sylvie says. 'You're almost there!'

But 'almost there' seems to last forever. Clare looks drained, exhausted. She slumps, defeated, against the foot of the bed.

'Too tired,' she whimpers. I want to shout at Sylvie and the midwife, scream at everyone to do something, fast, because it's clear to me that Clare has had enough. She needs help, medicine, doctors, something to put an end to all this. Instead, she opens her eyes and pulls one last effort from somewhere.

'I need to push,' she says, and the midwife does a quick check and tells her to go with it. The contractions are stronger still now, and Clare pushes down with each one, her face scrunched up with the effort.

'You're doing great,' the midwife tells Clare. 'I can see the baby's head. One more push . . .'

She goes to the door and calls for the doctor. He slips into the room soundlessly, moving about quietly, working with the midwife. In the brief rests between contractions, Clare seems to drift.

'Scarlett?' she murmurs. 'Are you there?'

'I'm here,' I tell her.

Then her face crumples and darkens, and she's pushing again. 'Ynnnuughhh . . .' she groans.

'Almost,' the midwife says encouragingly. 'One more, one more . . .'

Clare groans and pants again and suddenly the midwife is cradling a tiny, purple-pink baby, sticky with blood and greasy white stuff. The doctor bends over the baby, blocking my view.

'Buzz for paediatrics,' he says quietly, and the youngest nurse bustles out, blank-faced. Then there's a tiny, gasping cry like a cat yowling, and Clare's eyes fill with tears.

'You have a baby daughter,' the doctor says, and the baby is wrapped in a soft white blanket and laid on Clare's tummy for a moment. She's tiny, her face crumpled up as though she's angry at the world.

'Hey, hey,' I whisper. I touch her tiny clenched fist with one finger. She grabs on to it, and opens her milky-blue eyes wide at me. She's the most beautiful creature I've ever seen. Suddenly it's hard to focus. My eyes mist, and fat, salty tears roll slowly down my cheeks. I've never felt so happy before, so full of love, so much a part of things.

Then everything changes. Sylvie is behind me, pulling me back from the bedside. The young nurse is back, a woman doctor in tow.

'Let's get this young lady checked over for you,' the new doctor says smoothly, lifting the baby from Clare's arms. 'She's come along a little sooner than expected, so we'd like to keep an eye on her, make sure she's breathing properly.'

'Breathing?' Clare asks, alarmed.

'Just a few tests,' the doctor says gently. She tucks my brand-new sister inside a crib trolley and wheels her away, out of the hospital delivery room and down the corridor to special care.

'What's happening?' I ask Sylvie. 'Where are they taking her?'

Sylvie slips an arm round me and leads me to

the door. 'She's five weeks early,' she reminds me. 'She'll need some extra help for a while. It'll be OK, Scarlett, wait and see – your sister's going to be fine.'

I look over my shoulder and see Clare, leaning back against the pillows at last, crying softly. It just about breaks my heart.

Ed and Sylvie promise they'll stay with me until Dad and Holly arrive.

'When did you last eat?' Ed wants to know, and when I think about it I realize I've had nothing since breakfast. Sylvie flings an arm round me and the three of us head off to find the hospital canteen.

'I could murder some fried chicken and whipped potatoes,' Ed says. 'And some real coffee, not that stuff from the machine.'

'I don't care what it is,' Sylvie laughs, 'as long as it's good. Delivering babies is hard work, huh, Scarlett?'

'Mmm,' I say. 'Look, d'you mind if I see you in there? I need to find a phone box.'

'Use my cellphone,' Ed says.

'OK. Thanks, Ed. I'll see you both in a minute.'

They walk off down the corridor, following the signs to the canteen, and I sink down into a blue vinyl chair in another waiting area, outside a different ward. I punch the numbers in, press call and wait.

'Hello?' Alima's clipped voice responds. 'This is Sara Murray's secretary. What can I do for you?'

'I need to speak to my mum,' I say. 'It's urgent.'

'Scarlett?' Alima squeaks. 'Great to hear from you! Putting you right through . . .'

I blink. Alima has never put me right through to Mum before, not in living memory.

'Scarlett?' Mum's voice sounds high-pitched and strained. 'Sweetheart, is that you?'

'Mum,' I say.

'Scarlett, I'm so glad you called me at last, I've missed you terribly,' she babbles. 'Did you get my phone messages? I'm not sure your dad's been passing them on. Did you get my letters?'

'I got them,' I say shortly. 'All the messages, all the letters.'

'I see.' Mum clears her throat. 'That's OK then. I was just worried, Scarlett. Connemara is *so* far away. You were right, darling, I never should have made you go. I mean, you were never going to fit in, were you, not with them. You belong with me. I should have listened –'

'Mum,' I interrupt. 'Listen *now*. Clare's had a fall. She's had her baby early, five weeks early, and the doctors have taken it away to the special care unit and Ed and Sylvie are looking after me, but nobody actually knows what's happening. Clare's crying and Dad's not here, and . . .'

'And what, darling?' Mum asks.

A noise that's somewhere between a gasp and a howl leaks out of my mouth, and I know I can't hold it together for much longer. I can taste tears again, wet and salty, sliding down my face. What do I want of her anyway? I want her to be here, right now, to wrap me in her arms and wipe away my tears and make everything all right again. Like *that's* ever going to happen.

'Doesn't matter,' I say into the mobile. 'Bye, Mum.'

30

It's past midnight. Holly is asleep on a squashy blue vinyl chair beside me, her head resting on my shoulder. One of her mouse-brown plaits curls down round my arm like a snake.

Clare is sleeping in the maternity ward just along the corridor, and Dad is keeping his own night vigil in the special care unit nearby. My new little sister lies in an incubator, a tiny, angry doll. She looks like she could break at any minute. She is hooked up to tubes and drips and ventilators, and when I saw her I raked the dent in my tongue against my teeth and blinked back tears. I wanted to rip out the tubes and wires, lift her up and hold her tight, but I knew I couldn't.

I left Dad sitting with his face against the incubator, his hand inside one of the portholes, one curled finger resting against the baby's clenched fist while the doctors and nurses move silently around him.

Ed and Sylvie went hours ago, back to the real

world. They left me with a scribbled address (somewhere in Ohio) and promises that everything was going to be fine, and that we were to keep in touch and come visit some day, the whole family, baby included.

I shift around on my seat, letting Holly's head slip down towards my lap. She moans a little, pulls an arm across her eyes to block out the light. The minute hand on the wall clock jerks round in slow motion.

'Scarlett?' a voice says.

I turn, expecting to see the kind-faced nurse who brought me a hot chocolate earlier on, but the figure in the corridor is not a nurse. She's small and slim, with blonde hair piled up in a messy bun and a blue skirt-suit and impossibly high-heeled, pointy shoes. She looks tired and creased and slightly uncertain, standing there in the half-light.

'Mum?' I say. 'Mum, what are you doing here?'

Mum hugs me so tightly it feels like she's holding me together. When somebody holds you that tight, it feels safe — safe enough to let yourself fall to pieces. The tears come again, tears for Clare and Dad and my new baby sister wired up to monitors and machines and feeding tubes in the bright, warm room along the corridor. Tears for myself and the mess I've made of things.

'Scarlett,' Mum whispers into my hair. 'It's all right. It's all right.'

When I'm done with crying, she wipes my eyes and strokes my cheeks and I become aware of Holly, staring at us wide-eyed from the blue vinyl seats.

'It's OK,' I tell her. 'It's OK, Holls, really. This is my mum.'

'Hi, Holly,' Mum says to her politely, offering a hand to shake. 'I'm pleased to meet you at last. Let's find Chris, shall we?'

Mum takes charge. She tells Dad that Holly and I are exhausted, and offers to take us back to the cottage to get some sleep. 'I'll bring them back in the morning, when they've had some rest and some breakfast and a change of clothes,' she says. 'They can't stay here all night.'

'I'm not leaving Clare,' Dad says defensively. 'I'm not going anywhere until I know the baby's going to be OK.'

'Of course not,' Mum says. 'You're needed here. I'll take the girls – I got a hire car at the airport, and Scarlett can show me the way. Ring me in the morning, let me know what's happening.'

'The phone at the cottage is broken,' I remember.

Mum shrugs. 'Well, you've got my mobile number, Chris. Call me first thing.'

'I will,' Dad says. 'Thanks.'

'No problem,' Mum says. 'Come on, girls.'

We drive through the night in Mum's hire car, Holly fast asleep on the back seat, me wide awake, wired, fear running through me. I can't stop thinking about my new sister, tiny, frail and raw, not quite ready for the world. I wish I'd found a way to tell her to hang on, give it a chance.

The drive back takes forever because we don't have a map and the signposts are kind of crazy, but finally we get to Kilimoor and I know the way from there well enough.

Mum lifts Holly out of the car and scoops her up, brown legs dangling, to carry her in. The chickens rustle anxiously from the branches of the apple tree because nobody was around to shut them in the henhouse. The front door is unlocked, the lights blazing. The power cut is clearly over. Apart from that, the cottage is just the way we left it, the kitchen table heaped with fabric, the stepladder still propped up into the open attic hatch as we edge carefully past to Holly's room.

I pull the pink quilt back and Mum lowers Holly down gently, easing off her shoes, tucking the cover up around her chin. I drop a kiss on to her forehead, and see the look of surprise flicker across Mum's face. I draw the curtains and switch off the light as we leave the room.

Out on the landing, Mum folds the ladder and pulls the hatch closed while I gather up the little dresses still scattered across the floorboards. If Mum recognizes them, she doesn't say so.

She carries the stepladder downstairs, finds the back porch and props it inside, puts the kettle on, sweeps the mounds of scrap fabric off the table and into Clare's scrap-bag. I catch the corner of the cot quilt and rescue it, spreading the patchwork out across the table.

'Clare was making a cot quilt,' I tell Mum. 'She never finished it.'

Mum strokes a hand across the quilt, smoothing the surface, tracing the pattern of bright stitching that decorates each jigsaw join. 'Plenty of time for that,' she says softly. 'We can take it in to the hospital, tomorrow – Clare can work on it there if she's feeling up to it. Or maybe we could do a little bit . . .'

'Could we?' I ask. 'I'd like that, Mum. Thanks.'

'OK, sweetheart.' Mum smiles. 'No problem. But right now, you need to sleep. Bed, Scarlett. And don't worry – it'll all look better in the morning.'

I pause halfway up the stairs, looking down. 'Mum? You must have caught the first plane out here after I spoke to you this afternoon.'

'Ah,' she says, smiling. 'Alima made the

reservations over the phone. There were no late flights to Knock, but we found one going from Luton to Galway, and I took a taxi to the airport. The flight was on time, so it was just a case of hiring a car once I got there . . .'

'What will your boss say?' I ask.

'Couldn't care less,' Mum says. 'I work long enough hours for that firm – they don't own me.'

I raise an eyebrow. 'Mum, what exactly made you decide to come?'

She looks up, smiling. 'Easy,' she tells me. 'You needed me, Scarlett. Simple as that.'

I dream of Kian and Midnight and hazy afternoons by the loughside, holding hands beneath the wishing tree, riding along the ridges at sunset. I wake early, but not to a hail of gravel.

Kian is gone, just when I needed him most.

I dress quickly, grabbing my fluffy rucksack, stuffing in a few bits and pieces. I creep downstairs, past the squashy old sofa where Mum is sleeping, wrapped in one of Clare's patchwork throws. I dip a hand into Clare's scrap-bag, fishing out the dressmaking shears. I drop them into my rucksack, then open the door and slip outside.

The air is clean and fresh, and the grass is sprinkled with dew. In the hedge beside the gate, a dozen little spiders' webs shimmer. I walk down the lane, through the woods, to where the lough is sleeping beneath a soft blanket of mist. I sit down on a rock, empty my rucksack out on to the stones. Three red dresses, Clare's dressmaking shears.

I pick up the scissors and chop the skirt of the

red velvet party dress away from the waistband. I slice down one seam, snipping the skirt's soft fabric into strips of raggedy scarlet. I do the same with the crinkly silk dress and the rich red cotton with the embroidered hem, then I gather the pile of rags up in my arms and take them over to the wishing tree.

I tie them on to the branches, one by one, making wish after wish for my new baby sister until the tree is filled with red rags, fluttering scraps of scarlet, crimson, cerise. Then I sink down on to the grass and rest my back against the tree, looking out at the mist and the lough.

The rider comes out of the mist, at a canter, slowing as he reaches the tip of the lough, reining in the big black horse, turning him so that the pair splash along towards me through the shallows. My heart races.

Kian and Midnight stop a few metres in front of me. Midnight scuffs at the grass, snorting and shaking his head. Kian just sits astride him, brown hands knotted into the horse's mane, face half hidden behind a soft fall of dark hair.

'Where were you?' I ask, surprised at the anger in my voice. 'Where were you yesterday?'

Kian slides down from Midnight's back and turns to me. 'You know where I was,' he replies. 'I had to find my dad, let him know I was OK.'

'But you promised!' I fling at him. 'You lied to me! I needed you, and you weren't here.'

Kian drops down into the long grass beside me, hugging his knees in faded jeans. His tanned arms glint with little golden hairs, and the plaited leather bracelets on his wrists drop down over his hands, revealing a sliver of paler skin.

'Looks like you managed OK,' he says carefully.

'What would you know?' I protest. 'Yesterday was awful. Clare fell and went into labour early, and the storm knocked our phone out so we couldn't ring for help. I looked for you everywhere, but you weren't around!'

Kian rakes a hand over his face, pushing the hair back. His eyes look shadowed, haunted, like the eyes of the boy in the photograph yesterday. 'Is she OK now?' he asks softly. 'Clare, and the baby?'

'What do *you* care?' I cry, ashamed at how childish that sounds. 'Everything's messed up. My baby sister is in special care, and Clare won't stop crying and Dad looks so lost . . .'

Kian lets out a long, ragged breath. 'I do care, Scarlett,' he says. 'More than you know. My mum died in Castlebar Hospital, this time last year.'

That stops me. 'Your mum *died*?' I echo.

Kian nods. 'She had cancer – by the time she found out, it was too far gone to do anything, and

Mum was never one for doctors or hospitals anyway. We came out here, the whole family, my uncles and aunts, all of us. We stayed by the lough, did a bit of casual work for the local farmers, swam in the lough, ate rabbit stew. We partied every night, lit fires, told stories, danced, played music. Mum used to sing – she had the loveliest voice. We made the most of last summer, lived it one day at a time.'

'The travellers by the lough,' I whisper. 'Holly and Ros told me about it – big shiny caravans and horses and dogs. That was you?'

'That was us. Your cottage was just up the lane, so of course Holly would have known we were there. That's why I couldn't risk meeting her at the lough the other week – things would have got complicated.'

'That's how you knew about my dad, that first night at the lough,' I whisper. 'That's how you knew where I lived.'

'That's how.'

'What – what happened? About your mum?'

'We pretended nothing was wrong,' Kian says. 'We pretended, right up until the point when we couldn't pretend any more. Then it fell apart. Mum was too ill, in too much pain. My dad couldn't stand it – she begged him not to, but he drove her to Castlebar, to the hospital. We moved on, found a council site in the town, stayed there a while so we could visit her. But, Scarlett, she never came home.'

Kian makes a weird, gasping sound and covers his face. I can see his shoulders trembling slightly. I reach out to touch his hair, his face.

'I'm sorry, Kian,' I whisper. 'I didn't know.'

He pulls me close and we hold each other gently, cheeks touching, arms wrapped softly round each other as though we're each holding something very fragile, very special. I want to stay like that forever, feeling Kian's warm breath against my neck, the slight jut of his cheekbone against mine, a strand of his black hair blown across my lips by the soft breeze.

Then he sniffs and smiles and wipes his eyes on his sleeve, and we move apart awkwardly, still holding hands. Kian lets his head fall back against the hazel tree.

'Dad couldn't face travelling for a while,' he tells me. 'We went to Dublin, parked up on a permanent site. I went to school. It was bad – I didn't fit in and I couldn't get over Mum. I truanted a lot, and as soon as the warm weather started, I took Midnight and headed out here. I needed to be on my own, think things through. I needed to be here. I guess they've been looking for me ever since.'

I shut my eyes, guilt-stricken. 'I told them I'd

never seen you,' I say, remembering. 'I sent them away.'

Kian shrugs. 'They didn't go far – there's a place we used to like, on the coast to the south, right by the ocean. I rode out yesterday morning and found them there. We did some talking, sorted some stuff out. I think it's going to be OK.'

'I'm glad,' I say. 'I'm sorry I got angry, Kian. I thought I'd never see you again.'

'You were always going to see me again.' He grins. 'I had a promise to keep, didn't I?'

Neither of us point out that it was a promise to say goodbye.

'I'm sorry I wasn't here for you, yesterday,' he says. 'Do you think she'll be OK? Clare's baby?'

'I think she will,' I whisper. 'I hope so, anyway. They're doing all they can to help her.'

Kian's fingers stroke away tears, play with my hair. I can feel his soft breath on my cheek.

'Know what?' he says. 'I'm going to miss you. The first day I rode into Kilimoor, looking for supplies, the village was going crazy about some mad English girl who'd marched out of school and made for the hills. When we met up, later, right by the wishing tree, it seemed like it was meant to happen. I've had the best summer, Scarlett. I thought it'd be the worst, but you made it into the best, OK? I'll never forget that.'

It feels like a dream is falling to pieces right in front of me. My eyes are gritty with tears, showing me a world that's blurred and hazy.

'You're going back to your family, aren't you?' I ask.

'I have to, Scarlett,' he says. 'It's where I belong. I've felt like I was on my own for a long time now, but I'm not – none of us are. Families are never perfect, Scarlett, but you have to hold on to them. They're a part of you.'

I think of Mum, striding through the hospital corridors last night, brisk, efficient, taking charge. I had never been so happy to see anybody in my whole life.

'Maybe you're right,' I tell him.

'Hey,' he laughs. 'I'm always right, OK?'

He kisses me then, his lips soft and gentle and salty with tears, and I know he's saying goodbye.

'We'll meet again,' Kian says. 'I promise.'

I put a finger to his lips. 'Shhh,' I warn him. 'You're not so good at promises, remember.'

'Ah, you'll see,' he says. He takes a braided black bracelet off his wrist and ties it gently round mine, letting the ends dangle. 'Just don't forget me, that's all.'

He gets to his feet and just when I think he's going to walk away he turns and reaches up to the hazel tree, grabbing on to a branch.

'Any of those wishes for me?' he asks.

'Maybe one or two.'

He unties one of the scarlet rags and rakes a hand through his untidy hair before using the rag to tie it back. Then he whistles for Midnight and takes him by the bridle, and the two of them walk away slowly along the silver shore of the lough until they're lost from sight in the mist and the dawn and the blur of my tears.

When I get back to the cottage, Mum is in the garden in a borrowed kimono wrap, collecting eggs from underneath the rose bushes. She's bare-legged but wearing her trademark spike heels, which keep sinking into the grass and giving her a lopsided, slightly unsteady look. Her long hair is loose and uncombed, and she's singing to herself as she drifts about the garden.

My mum never sings. She looks up and stops in her tracks, smiling softly, as though she hasn't seen me for a long, long time. Apart from last night, I guess she hasn't.

'Scarlett,' she says. 'Your dad rang. The baby's had a good night, and the doctors have taken her off the ventilator. That's great news, isn't it?'

'She's OK?' I gasp. 'She's out of special care?'

'She's fine,' Mum confirms. 'I think they'll keep her in special care for a while, just to be on the safe side, but she's out of danger. What a relief!'

I never thought she'd care.

'Poor Clare,' she says. 'Poor Chris. If anything had happened to that baby . . .' She slips an arm round my shoulders and we go inside, and I want to shout and sing and dance with relief because my new baby sister is going to be OK, after all.

I start with the shouting. 'Holly!' I yell. 'Holly, wake up! The baby's out of danger! Everything's going to be fine!'

Holly pads down the stairs, bleary-eyed, still wearing yesterday's crumpled clothes. I take her hands and waltz her round the kitchen until she's wide awake and laughing, and we flop down at the kitchen table just as Mum sets down plates of scrambled eggs, baked beans, grilled mushrooms and tomatoes. It's actually veggie. For once, my mum is paying attention.

She hacks into one of Clare's granary loaves, producing a mound of crumbling brown bricks. She butters one and takes a bite. 'Ugh,' she groans. 'What *is* that, wholemeal sawdust? Give me ciabatta any day.'

Just when I'm starting to think my mum has taken a crash course in full-on, earth-mother, knit-your-own-lentils sweetness and light, she comes over all snooty city girl.

I guess I kind of like her like that.

*

Mum stays on at the cottage for a fortnight, while Dad and Clare camp out at the hopsital, waiting for the moment the doctors will declare my new baby sister is well enough to come home.

Mum doesn't moan about missing work, she just calls in and says it's an emergency and that she's owed a whole raft of holidays anyhow, might as well take them now. She helps Holly and me to decorate the sky-blue bedroom with sparkly stars and a crescent moon painted in silver acrylic paint. We paint a wide, arching rainbow that stretches from one corner of the room to another. When my new baby sister looks up from her cot, she'll see stars to wish on, a moon to soothe her to sleep, a slice of rainbow to remind her that magic is always just round the corner.

I move my bed into Holly's room, and hey, it's not so bad. Seriously.

We finish the cot quilt, too, Mum and Holly and me. We add a border of red patches round Clare's quilt, a jigsaw of scarlet, crimson and bright vermilion red, snipped from the remaining dresses in the attic. We all take turns at patching the pieces together, stitching them down, decorating the joins with zigzag or chain stitch or French knots in bright, contrasting threads. I've stitched my love into that quilt, my hopes and dreams for my new baby sister.

We take it along to the hospital and give it to Clare, who hugs us all, even Mum, and puts the quilt at the end of the baby's incubator. My new baby sister kicks her legs and opens her eyes wide and when I put my hand in through the porthole in the side of the plastic cot, she takes my finger in her tiny fist and squeezes, and I know that she loves me and guess what, I love her back, now, always, forever, no questions asked.

Clare sits in a comfy chair in the visitors' room beside the special care unit, watching the baby through the glass partition and leafing through a book on names.

'I'd like a Gaelic name,' Clare muses. 'The trouble is, there are so many lovely ones and it's hard to know which one is right.'

'Aislinn,' Dad offers. 'It means dream, vision, inspiration. That would fit.'

'Or Etain,' Holly says. 'That means shining one. What d'you think?'

Clare frowns. 'I'm not sure,' she says. 'What about Kiara? Small and dark, that means.'

I take the book from Clare, scanning the page until I find what I'm looking for. I read it, and my eyes mist over.

'Got one, Scarlett?' Dad asks, but I shake my head.

The name I've found is not for my baby sister. It's Kian, and it means ancient, enduring, magical.

Clare gets up and wanders over to the glass partition. 'Maybe an old Irish name is too grand, too fancy, for such a little girl,' she muses. 'Maybe we're looking in the wrong place.'

She reaches out to touch the vase of flowers on the wide window sill, gathered fresh this afternoon from the cottage garden. Her fingers trace the velvet petals of deep pink roses, raggedy shasta daisies, tall, pale, regal lilies. At the back, for foliage and for luck, are a few branches of hazel from the wishing tree, with soft green leaves and tiny, budding nuts clustered in groups of three.

'Hazel,' Clare says slowly. 'I think her name is . . . Hazel.'

My heart thumps.

'Hazel,' Dad repeats. 'Hazel, Holly and Scarlett . . . it feels right, somehow. I like it.'

And after two weeks in hospital, my baby sister Hazel comes home. She lies in her cot and twists her beautiful cot quilt between her fists and gazes at the stars and the moon and the rainbow up above her. Overnight, the cottage smells of baby powder and wet wipes and other, dodgier, nappy-type aromas.

Mum books her plane ticket home, and we all drive to Knock to wave her off.

'I'll never be able to thank you enough,' Clare tells her. 'You've been a star. Looking after the girls, keeping the cottage and the garden in order, running everyone up and down to the hospital. Even keeping the Internet soap orders ticking over! Thanks, Sara.'

The two women hug, and I'm sure I see Mum wipe her eye. She must have a speck of dust in it.

'We really are grateful,' Dad adds. 'We couldn't have managed without you.'

'My pleasure,' Mum sniffs. 'It was a holiday for me.'

Holly doesn't waste words, she just hurls herself at Mum and hugs her tightly, and then it's down to me. I look at Mum and I know that there's no speck of dust that could account for the fat, shiny tears running down her cheeks.

'Sweetheart, I'll miss you,' she whispers.

'I'll miss you too.'

It feels like I'm being torn in two all over again, and even though it was Mum who sent me away to Ireland, it feels like we're sending her away now. She looks little and lost, standing in the airport check-in queue with one measly overnight bag and nothing and nobody to go home to. I fling my arms round her and I hold her tightly.

'I'm sorry, Scarlett,' she says into my hair. 'I'm so, so sorry for everything. I handled it all wrong, the break-up. I was a mess, and I wasn't there for you. I'm sorry.'

'It doesn't matter,' I murmur, because it doesn't, not any more. 'We both messed up, didn't we?'

'Big style,' Mum laughs. 'It's a talent we have.'

'A skill,' I agree. 'But hey, we're learning, aren't we? We'll get through.'

'I love you, Scarlett,' she tells me. 'Always. Any time you want to come home, just let me know. It'll be different now, I promise you. We can work things out together – schools, friends, rules. Can't we?'

'Maybe, Mum,' I tell her. 'Who knows?'

Maybe.

I stay in Connemara till the end of the summer. I watch my baby sister grow, see her cheeks flush pink from lying out in the garden on her patchwork cot quilt, kicking her legs. I watch her learn to focus her eyes, form her tiny rosebud mouth into a smile meant just for me.

In the day, I hook up with Ros and Matty and sometimes Kevin Fahey, the shy boy who wants to be a priest. He's no pin-up, no dreamboy, but he's fun. He's a friend, and I need all the friends I can get.

At night, I lie awake talking to Holly. I listen to her chatter, I tell her about my day, I tell her, again and again, how lucky I am to have her and Hazel. 'We're connected,' I tell her. 'Bound together, no matter what. Sisters, OK?'

'Sisters.' Holly sighs in the dark, and slips into sleep.

But when Dad starts talking about schools again, I know it's time to move on.

'You've made friends,' Dad tells me. 'You'll fit into the school at Westport, no problem now, the same way you've fitted in with us. It's a terrific school, and you'll get the chance to really stretch yourself –'

'No, Dad,' I say.

'No?' he falters. 'Well, I'm certain you'd have no problems, Scarlett. You're a different girl these days. The anger and the hurt and the fear, it's just gone, hasn't it? But if you'd rather stick with the home-schooling . . .'

'I'm sorry, Dad,' I tell him. 'It hurts like crazy, but I know it's the right thing to do. I love you and Clare, I love Holly and Hazel. I love it here, more than anything. But I'm going home – to Mum.'

I fall into London life as if I've never left, except of course I am different now, stronger. I've got nothing to prove.

I march along the pavement from the tube station at the Angel, flat Mary Jane shoes kicking

219

through the litter. My tights are bottle green, my skirt is knee-length and pleated, my green blazer is trimmed with gold cord, adorned with an embroidered badge that says something in Latin about aiming high and reaching the stars.

Luckily, green goes pretty well with ketchup-red hair.

My new school is strict, but I'm not fighting any more, so that doesn't matter. I'm not a perfect, grade-A student, but I get good marks in English and art and history and drama, and I haven't wasted too much time in the Head's office or the detention room. I've made some friends, real friends, the kind who'd never think of offering you ciggies in the school loo or daring you to nick an eye pencil from Boots. They're cool.

Things are better with Mum and me too. She doesn't work such long hours these days, and we take time out to talk and find out what's going on with each other. We still lose it sometimes – we're both hot-tempered, I guess, but we're working on it. Seriously, it's a whole lot better.

For my birthday, Mum got me the best present ever – a baby rabbit. I called her Smudge and she's a house rabbit – she gets to mooch around the flat and we've even trained her to use a litter tray. Dad called too, and asked me what I wanted, and when I told him, he rang round a few places and found me riding lessons, right here in the centre of London. It's not like riding bareback on Midnight along the shores of Lough Choill, but it's pretty cool all the same.

I miss Dad and Clare and Holly and Hazel, but I'm going back at Easter, and for part of the summer holidays too. I'm really looking forward to that.

I miss Kian too, of course, and that's way harder. There was hardly a day, over those five weeks, that we didn't see each other. We talked, we laughed, we lazed around in the sun. We held hands and flirted and once, just once, we kissed, a sad, lingering kiss that tasted of salt and tears. All I have to remember him are memories, and a little black braided bracelet that stays on my wrist night and day.

Sometimes, I catch a glimpse of a boy who looks like Kian, the same wild black hair, the same scruffy-chic clothes and lazy, ambling stride. Then the boy turns round and of course he's nothing like Kian. How could he be?

It's like it never happened, and that's the toughest thing of all. Magic. Yeah, right.

I turn into the driveway, crunch my way up the path and punch in the door code. I run up the stairs and on to the landing and then it hits me, suddenly, the smell of wild mint, in London, in December.

It makes my heart race, it makes my throat ache.

Outside the door to our flat is a pair of broken-up old sandals, the scarily high wedge heels encrusted with moss. Lying against one sandal are a couple of tiny wild strawberries and a hazel twig with catkins and nuts on the same branch. A pair of faded, swirly sandals, curls of ivy where the ribbons should be? Strawberries, in December? Catkins and nuts on the same branch? Suddenly, I'm certain there's someone behind me. I whirl round but there's nobody there, just the empty landing and the silent staircase and the lingering smell of wild mint.

I pick up the sandals, the strawberries and the hazel branch, and I turn the key in the lock and go inside.

Who can *melt* an ice-cream heart?

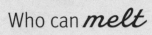

Sundae Girl

Turn the page for a *sweet treat* …

Don't get me wrong, I love my family. I live with Gran, Grandad, Mum and Toto in a semi-detached house in a street called Pine Tree Avenue. There are no pine trees anywhere around, except now, in December, when they are in every window, decorated with fairy lights and tinsel.

At this time of year, Grandad likes to give his name and address as Patrick Reilly, 211 Christmas Tree Avenue. This causes problems with banks, taxi drivers, delivery firms and postmen. The fact that he has a full white beard and a figure like Santa Claus does not help matters.

Gran used to be a calming influence on him, but for a few years now she's had Alzheimer's disease – Old-Timer's Disease, Grandad calls it. She's not in any kind of pain, but she forgets stuff, like names and dates and even how to get dressed properly. Not long ago, she went missing and we tracked her down in Tesco, still in her dressing gown, loading a trolley with kiwi fruit and telling an anxious shelf-stacker how to knit an Aran jumper.

I remember when Gran was the one who held the house together, the one who baked fresh scones if I brought a friend over from school, jam tarts on a Sunday. She used to make me beautiful jumpers with stripes or Fair Isle patterns, and hats and mittens and scarves and shawls for friends and relatives and neighbours. Now, it's just the scarves, and nobody really wants them. They are metres long and full of lumps and holes.

It should be Mum looking after Gran and Grandad, looking after me, but she just isn't that kind of person. She is forty-four years old, going on fourteen. Sometimes she's gorgeous and glamorous and funny. Sometimes she really is not.

In the evenings, she sits at the piano hammering out grim old Irish songs that make you want to cry into your cocoa, telling anyone who'll listen about her glory days as a singer. 'I could have been a star,' she likes to tell me. 'I won the weekly talent contest at Butlins in Clacton-on-Sea in 1981, and I often played the piano at the Irish centre. Very popular, I was. Then I met your dad, Jude, and that was the end of that.'

Now Mum works part-time in the hairdresser's on the corner, a salon called Chop Suey after its owner, Sue. Often, people ring up to order egg-fried rice and chicken noodles, and get annoyed when offered blonde highlights instead.

And Toto? He's our dog, a tall, languid Afghan hound with flowing strawberry-blonde hair. He is very beautiful, but very stupid. The dogs' home told us he was a pedigree, but that he'd run away from home so often his owner despaired of him. This appealed to Grandad, who likes a challenge.

Toto has never run away from us, perhaps because Mum brushes his hair and scooshes him with leave-in conditioner every day, or perhaps because Grandad buys him gory old bones from the butcher and walks him for miles every morning and night.

'Well,' Grandad announces, the morning after Parents' Night. 'Your teachers were full of praise, Jude. Well done.'

'Yes, well done,' Mum agrees, sipping her black coffee while the rest of us pick at our cornflakes. 'You take after me. I was always good at school too, you know.'

'Fiddlesticks!' says Gran, and Mum shoots her an angry look.

'What?' she asks, blinking sweetly, smoothing the tea-stained green scarf out across the table and brushing off the remnants of last night's flapjack crumbs. 'I dropped a stitch, that's all.'

Mum frowns and goes back to her coffee.

'I don't know what your father thinks he was doing there,' she says darkly. 'Dressed in that – that *catsuit* thing too. Whatever must your teachers have thought?'

'He had an OAP party to go to,' I say lightly. 'He was going straight on there after the school.'

'Why does he have to embarrass us like that?' Mum sulks.

'I thought you liked all that showbiz stuff,' Grandad reminds her. 'And you were just as bad yourself in the beginning, admit it! White PVC knee-boots, black minidress, blonde beehive hair . . .'

When Mum and Dad first met, Dad was in a Beatles tribute band called the Fab Four. He was supposed to be Paul McCartney – I've seen the pictures. Mum got into that whole dressing-up thing, and the band let her fill in as backing singer sometimes. Sadly, she wasn't very good, so any dreams of a career pretending to be a young Lulu or Cilla Black bit the dust pretty quickly.

'I grew out of it,' Mum says sharply. '*He* just got fat and had to give up the Fab Four to become an Elvis lookalike. How sad is that?'

'He makes a living,' I point out, thinking of the weekly cheque he sends Mum to help pay for my shoes, my winter coat, my piano lessons.

'Well, anyway, he shouldn't lurk about at Jude's Parents' Night. What did he think he was *doing*?'

'The same as us,' Grandad sighs. 'I asked him to come. He has a right, Rose – she's his daughter too.'

Mum scowls. 'I wish she wasn't.'

'You can't change it, love,' Grandad says. 'It's done. Blood is thicker than water.'

I've heard it all a million times before, but I still don't get it. Mum left Dad, all those years ago. She cancelled the wedding and scooped me into a rickety pram with a suitcase balanced on top, and she marched back home to Gran and Grandad's. It was her decision to leave – so why is she still angry, twelve years on? Beats me.

I finish my cornflakes, rifle through the stuff on the clothes airer for my gym kit.

Mum is brushing out Gran's long grey hair. Before she got ill, Gran had the most fantastic hair – she'd wear it up, in a French pleat or a wispy bun, or knotted loosely with a bright silk scarf tied round it. Now, she forgets to even brush it, so Mum does it, smoothing it, plaiting it, pinning the braids up across her head so she looks like the picture on the cover of a book I once read. Heidi, but with wrinkles.

'Ah, Molly,' Grandad sighs. 'My sweet Irish colleen.'

'Who's Molly?' Gran asks brightly. 'Do I know her?'

'You're Molly, pet,' Grandad says sadly. He stacks up the breakfast plates and dumps them into the sink.

'All I'm saying,' Mum huffs, 'is that if he insists on turning up at Jude's school, he should at least leave *that woman* behind.'

'Victoria is a lovely girl,' Grandad says firmly. Victoria is a bank clerk in Grandad's local branch. 'Very kind. And she's always been good to our Jude, hasn't she?'

Victoria is great, but Mum definitely doesn't want to hear that. Not this morning, and not from me. Unless I can tell her that Victoria eats raw liver for supper and tortures small animals as a hobby, my comments are not wanted here. I stay silent.

'That dreadful suit she was wearing,' Mum says. 'And her hair! Why can't she get it done professionally?'

'She looked very nice to me,' Grandad says.

'And that engagement ring was just *beautiful*,' Gran chips in.

Mum drops the hairbrush, and it clatters on to the floor. We all stare at Gran, eyes wide with horror, but she's gazing down at her knitting again, brows furrowed. She might as well be a million miles away.

Mum makes a kind of choking sound. 'Engagement ring?' she gasps. 'I didn't see an engagement ring. Did you?'

We shake our heads, stunned into silence.

'He wouldn't. Would he, Jude?'

'No,' I whisper, but I don't know, not really. Dad loves Victoria, I know that. She loves him. Why shouldn't they get married? But . . . wouldn't he tell me first?

'Take no notice of your gran,' Mum says boldly. 'She's always getting things mixed up. The very idea!'

I pick up my bag from the coat peg in the hall. Mum's right – Gran does get muddled up. Not this time, though. Something tells me that this time Gran's not muddled up at all.

Everyone is talking about the Green Scarf Incident from yesterday's Parents' Night. Kevin Carter's fateful fall has been transformed from something clumsy and embarrassing into something wonderful, heroic. Carter has a bandaged right arm and gets out of work for hours, until someone remembers he's left-handed.

By late afternoon, the true identity of the batty old couple with the green scarf at the centre of the action is at last revealed. Kristina Kowalski, glancing down at me like I'm something disgusting she just scraped off her spike-heeled shoe, is not impressed.

'You told Carter they were my *parents*,' she hisses. 'You sad little loser.'

'I . . . er . . . thought he was talking about someone else,' I bluff.

'Yeah, right,' Kristina says. 'And I do not have seven little sisters, OK? I'm an only child. Really, Jude, I pity you.'

She wiggles on up to the back of the English room and perches on Brendan Coyle's desk. Her skirt, another shrunk-in-the-wash special, slides up scarily to reveal acres of fake-tan thigh. Kristina Kowalski is the only girl I know who comes to school in December wearing high heels, ankle socks and a micro-mini. I hope she gets icicles on her bum.

'Ignore her,' Nuala O'Sullivan says, beside me. 'Everyone has grandparents. What's the big deal?'

'No big deal,' I sigh.

'And anyway, that thing with the scarf was a useful diversion.' Nuala grins. 'It took the heat off your dad. If Kristina ever finds out about him . . .'

'Don't. It doesn't bear thinking about.'

'Oh, Jude, you worry too much,' she laughs. She can afford to – she has a normal mum and dad with normal jobs and normal dress sense.

Miss Devlin sweeps into the classroom, a small, fierce whirlwind dressed entirely in navy blue. 'Miss Kowalski, back to your own seat,' she snaps. 'And Miss Kowalski – I wonder if you could remember to wear a skirt tomorrow? Knee-length, grey, regulation. If you forget yet again, perhaps I could find something in the lost-property cupboard for you?'

'No thanks, *Miss* Devlin,' Kristina replies. 'I'll remember.' She makes it sound like a threat.

We settle down to write an essay called 'School Uniform: For or Against?' I surprise myself by coming out in favour of knee-length grey skirts, stripy ties and hideous maroon blazers. In uniform, you can blend in, become invisible. You look just like everyone else . . . even if you're really not.

'I hate uniform,' Nuala whispers. 'Who wants to be a sheep?'

I do. I really, really do.

At the end of the lesson, we hand in our books and put our chairs up on the desks, because it's the end of the day. The bell rings out, but we never get away that lightly, not with Miss Devlin. St Joseph's is a Catholic school, and Miss Devlin is an old-style Catholic. She makes us join our hands, close our eyes and pray silently.

When the shuffling and coughing dies down, I pray for Gran and Grandad, Mum and Dad and Victoria and Toto. I pray that Gran was wrong, even though I'm not sure what's so scary about the idea of Dad getting married. It just is.

'Let us finish,' Miss Devlin says, 'by offering up a special prayer for Kevin Carter, so that his wrist heals quickly. For Brendan Coyle, so that he learns to stop wasting time in my lesson. And Kristina Kowalski, so that she finds her school skirt and her manners. We pray to St Jude – the patron saint of hopeless cases. Amen.'

There's a snort of laughter from Brendan Coyle and then we're dismissed, clattering down the stairs and out towards the school gates.

I'm halfway down the street when Kevin Carter skates up and gives me a high five with his bandaged hand.

'That prayer worked quickly,' I observe.

'Aw, it was just a scam. Thought I'd go for the sympathy vote. So, how come your parents named you after the patron saint of hopeless cases? That's a bit mean.'

'They didn't,' I say shortly. I've heard it all before, this stuff about St Jude, and I refuse to be bugged by it.

'So how come . . .'

'Dad named me after his favourite song,' I explain. 'It was a Beatles track called "Hey Jude". Mum didn't mind because her favourite film star was called Judy Garland. There were no saints involved, OK?'

'OK.' Kevin Carter nods, but seems in no hurry to move off. I walk on, and he skates along beside me, tripping occasionally on uneven paving stones.

'I wanted to say sorry,' he admits at last. 'About last night, y'know?'

'It's not your fault you're useless on Rollerblades.'

'Not about the fall,' he says. 'I mean, I am sorry about that, but . . . it was the laughing at your grandparents, really. I didn't realize.'

I raise one eyebrow. 'Doesn't matter,' I say. 'They are odd. That's just the way it is. Could have been worse.'

He could have clocked that Elvis was my dad.

'Was he really a championship boxer? Your grandad?'

Grandad worked for the post his whole life, but Kevin Carter's not to know that.

'Might have been.'

'OK. Well, I know you don't have seven little sisters – you're an only child, like Kristina. But the rest of the story . . . the bit about watching *Neighbours* with Martin Peploe from Year Nine. Was that you?'

I stare at Kevin Carter, amazed. He thinks I once sat on a sofa with Martin Peploe? I can feel myself going pink. It's the best compliment anyone ever gave me.

'You don't have to talk about it if you don't want.' Carter shrugs. 'Some things are private.'

'They are,' I agree.

'But I'd like you to know that I think Martin Peploe has excellent taste.'

Carter winks, scarily, and skates off down the road like someone just put a rocket down his trousers. He gets right down to the junction before colliding with a pillar box.

'I'm getting better,' he shouts over as I cross the street.

Better than what? I wonder, but I know what St Jude would say. Better than hopeless.

Dad lives in a little terraced house near the city centre. When I ring the doorbell, the chime plays 'Blue Suede Shoes'.

'Jude, sweetheart!' Dad says, opening the door in jeans and a T-shirt that says *Elvis Lives*. 'Come in, my little child-genius. Your teachers were pleased with you last night. Me and Vic were so proud!'

'Don't be daft,' I laugh. 'Thanks for coming, anyway.'

Now that it's over, I guess I *am* glad Dad and Victoria were there. I just wish they'd blended into the background a bit more.

'Didn't mind the white flares, did you?' Dad asks, reading my mind. 'I don't think anyone noticed.'

'Of course not.' White nylon catsuits with rhinestone-studded stand-up collars are all the rage among the parents at St Joseph's. 'How was the gig at the old folks' home?'

'Not bad,' Dad shrugs. 'They soon warmed up. Had them jiving round their Zimmer frames in the end, you know how it is.'

I do. I used to love going along to gigs with Dad. He is a very good Elvis impersonator, I'll give him that. He has the craziest clothes, the widest flares, the biggest quiff. He wiggles his hips and old ladies (and some young ones) squeal and roar with laughter. He works the crowd, crooning 'Love Me Tender' and gazing into the eyes of some old battleaxe, and next thing you know she's giggling like a teenager and blushing to the roots of her purple rinse.

Dad loves it, all this Elvis stuff, and his enthusiasm is catching. Except to me. These days, I am immune.

We drift through to the kitchen.

'Toast?' asks Dad, loading up the toaster and setting out the jam and butter.

'OK.'

We sit and eat toast that's dripping with butter and slathered with strawberry jam. It is a secret vice we have, the two of us. Dad reckons I must have inherited it from him, along with the black hair and freckles.

'So,' he says, crunching happily. 'How's school?'

'Great,' I lie brightly. 'How's work?'

'Busy. Always is, in the run-up to Christmas. I'm booked out – office parties, old folks' homes, discos, karaoke, the lot. Still, it should be fun!'

'Should be,' I echo.

'Jude, love,' Dad says. 'Is something bothering you?'

'No. At least . . . can I ask you a question?'

'Sure! Fire away.' Dad grins.

'Why did Mum leave you?'

I'm not sure where that came from, because actually I'm here to ask if he's getting married to Victoria. Digging up the dim and distant past is not part of the plan. Dad stares down at his toast crumbs, shell-shocked.

'Things didn't work out,' he tells me, which is all that anyone has ever been able to tell me. Suddenly, it just isn't enough.

'Why didn't they?' I push. 'Did you stop loving her? Did you have an affair?'

'No!' Dad sounds angry. 'Nothing like that, Jude. Perhaps you should ask your mum.'

'I'm asking you,' I remind him.

'Yes, you are.'

'So?'

'So . . . oh, Jude, we cared a lot about each other. We met after a Fab Four gig. We were together for years, having fun, out every night, touring with the band. Then you came along, and everything should have been perfect. We were planning to get married – a church wedding, a white dress for Rose, the lot.'

I want to remind him that weddings are meant to come before babies, but I bite my tongue. Instead I try to picture myself as the littlest bridesmaid ever, pink-faced and beaming in a dress full of frills.

'What went wrong?'

Dad sighs. 'Looking after a baby isn't easy. Your mum was a bit wiped out at first, she found it hard to cope. I was away a lot, with the band, so I couldn't help as much as I'd have liked. She started drinking. I mean, we'd always liked a drink, the two of us, so I didn't notice it to start with, but then I realized Rose was drinking in the day.

'You can't do that when you've got a baby to look after, Jude. I got scared. I started taking more and more time off from the band, to look after you, until finally they found someone else to take my place.'

Dad lets his shoulders sag, remembering.

'Go on,' I say quietly. I want to hear it all, now we've got started. It's my history, after all.

'We put the wedding off, till things got better,' Dad remembers. 'Only – well, they never did. I couldn't stand it, the way she was drinking, kidding herself that everything was fine. One day, we argued over breakfast. I poured all the drink in the house away, and Rose packed a suitcase and took you home to her parents.'

Mum left Dad because he wouldn't let her have whisky for breakfast. It's not what I imagined, but then again, it's not exactly a shock. Mum doesn't drink these days, but that's because the doctor says she can't. She's messed up her body with years and years of it, of drinking and weeping softly into the bottom of a whisky glass.

I always thought she drank because of Dad. Now I know it's because of *me*.

'Jude?' Dad is looking at me intently. 'You said you wanted to know. I'm sorry.'

'Me too.'

'I didn't want to let you go,' Dad says. 'It broke my heart, but I knew Molly and Patrick would look after you – and Rose, of course. It seemed like the best thing at the time.' He reaches out across the table and squeezes my hand.

'I always thought it was something *you* did,' I say shakily.

'So did I, Jude. So did I.'

When Victoria gets in from work, she finds us baking sponge cake from a dog-eared recipe book. Things have not gone well. I do not have

Gran's gift for baking, and Dad doesn't have the right kind of flour, the right amount of eggs, the right kind of sandwich tins. And we've eaten all the strawberry jam. We press on regardless, pouring the mixture into a non-stick loaf-tin, whipping up butter and icing sugar and cocoa powder to make buttercream icing to die for.

'Hi, Jude.' Victoria grins, chucking her jacket on the sofa and kicking off her shoes. 'Smells gorgeous. What's the occasion?'

'Oh, nothing much,' I say airily. 'We're just celebrating something.'

Victoria shoots a quizzical look at Dad, who pretends not to notice. 'So, what are we celebrating?' she asks again.

'Nothing important,' I tease. 'Just the fact that you're finally going to make an honest man of my dad!'

'You told her!' Victoria squeals. 'Oh, Jude, what do you think? Are you OK with it? Because if you think it's too soon . . .'

'Soon? You've been living together for six years!'

'I know, but if you'd rather we waited . . .'

'Victoria! I'm trying to tell you how happy I am. OK?'

'OK!' She flings her arms round me and hugs me tight, and I wonder how I ever could have thought this was a bad idea. Victoria and Dad are perfect for each other.

'Want to see the ring?' She blushes, showing me her left hand with the tiny diamond glinting. 'Isn't it beautiful?'

'Gorgeous,' I tell her.

'You're gorgeous,' Dad corrects me, putting an arm round each of us. 'My two gorgeous girls.'

Just then, the oven timer goes off and I dive for an oven glove to rescue the cake. I lift it out, golden brown, looking like a small, steaming housebrick with a worrying dent in the middle.

'It'll be fine once we've got the icing on,' Dad says doubtfully.

'Of course it will,' Victoria says kindly. 'What exactly is it, anyway?'

My mouth twitches, and Dad is unable to keep a straight face. Soon we're doubled up, laughing, and all I can do is point to the recipe book, the page splattered now with chocolate buttercream and bits of eggshell.

It's Victoria Sponge.

Which Chocolate Box Girl Are You?

Your perfect day would be spent . . .

a) visiting a busy vintage market
b) with your favourite canine companion on a long walk in the countryside
c) curled up on the sofa watching black-and-white movies with your boyfriend
d) window-shopping with your BFF
e) sipping frappuccinos in a hip city cafe

Your ideal boy is . . .

a) arty and sensitive
b) boy? No thanks!
c) a good listener . . . and a little bit quirky
d) polite and clever
e) good looking and popular – what other kind of boy is there?

Who's the first person you would tell about your new crush?

a) your sister – she knows everything about you
b) your pet cat . . . animals are great listeners
c) your BFF
d) your mum – she always has the best advice
e) no one. It's best not to trust anyone with a secret

Your favourite subject is . . .

a) history
b) science
c) creative writing
d) French
e) drama

Your school books are . . .

a) covered in paisley-print fabric
b) a bit muddy
c) filled with doodles
d) neat, tidy and full of good grades
e) rarely handed in on time

When you grow up you want to be . . .

a) an interior designer
b) a vet
c) a writer
d) a prima ballerina
e) famous

People always compliment your . . .

a) individuality. If anyone can pull it off you can!
b) caring nature – every creature deserves a bit of love
c) wild imagination . . . although it can get you into trouble sometimes
d) determination. Practice makes perfect
e) strong personality. You never let anyone stand in your way

Mostly As . . . *Skye*

Cool and eclectic, friends love your relaxed boho style and passion for all things quirky.

Mostly Bs . . . *Coco*

A real mother earth, but with your feet firmly on the ground, you're happiest in the great outdoors – accompanied by a whole menagerie of animal companions.

Mostly Cs . . . *Cherry*

'Daydreamer' is your middle name . . . Forever thinking up crazy stories and buzzing with new ideas, you always have an exciting tale to tell – you're allowed a bit of artistic licence, right?

Mostly Ds . . . *Summer*

Passionate and fun, you're determined to make your dreams come true . . . and your family and friends are behind you every step of the way.

Mostly Es . . . *Honey*

Popular, intimidating, lonely . . . everyone has a different idea about the 'real you'. Try opening up a bit more and you'll realize that friends are there to help you along the way.

A gorgeous new series by

Cathy Cassidy

The Chocolate Box GIRLS

Cherry:
Dark almond eyes, skin the colour of milky coffee, wild imagination, feisty, fun . . .

Skye:
Wavy blonde hair, blue eyes, smiley, individual, kind . . .

Summer:
Slim, graceful, pretty, loves to dance, determined, a girl with big dreams . . .

Honey:
Willowy, blonde, beautiful, arty and out of control, a rebel . . .

Coco:
Blue eyes, fair hair, freckles, a tomboy who loves animals and wants to change the world . . .

Each sister has a different story to tell, which will be your favourite?

Best Friends are there for you in the good times and the bad. They can keep a secret and understand the healing power of chocolate.

Best Friends make you laugh and make you happy. They are there when things go wrong, and never expect any thanks.

Best Friends are forever,

Best Friends Rock!

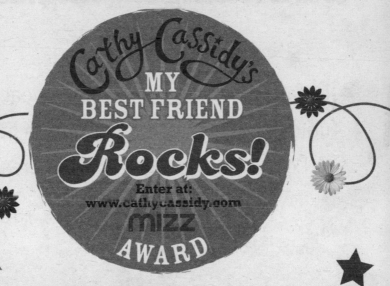

Cathy Cassidy's
MY
BEST FRIEND
Rocks!
Enter at:
www.cathycassidy.com
mizz
AWARD

Is your *Best Friend* one in a million?

Go to *www.cathycassidy.com* to find out how you can show your best friend how much you care